EMOTIONLESS

JAHQUEL J.

Published by Urban Chapters Publications
www.urbanchapterspublications.com

Contains explicit languages and adult themes
suitable for ages 16+

TEXT UCP TO 22828 TO SUBSCRIBE TO OUR MAILING LIST

If you would like to join our team, submit the first 3-4 chapters of your completed manuscript to

Submissions@UrbanChapterspublications.com

AUTHOR'S NOTES:

This is my attempt at a contemporary novel. My male character is from the hood, so he speaks like he's from the hood. However, he has a career and he's not in the streets. This book was so hard to write because it was a tad bit different than what I'm used to writing. I hope you all enjoy. If you're looking for a fast-paced book, skip this book. Things happen in this book the way I have planned them. I'm in love with Happy and Colt's story. For those looking for love, it's coming... right when you're least expecting it.

-Jahquel J.

To my love. The man who is responsible for the glow everyone says I have. It's so easy to write about love when you're being loved right. You make my heart dance when I'm around you. I love loving you. This year is a special anniversary. Not only is it two years that we've been married, but ten years since we've been together. To us, my King. I love you. Forever and ever.

-Boobie Kakes

SYNOPSIS

Galleria Stores is a huge chain of stores owned by Paul Galleria. Everyone who is anyone in Atlanta knows the Galleria family and their influence in Atlanta. Paul has three daughters – Jade, Kharisma & Happy Galleria. This is Happy's story.

Twenty-nine-year-old Happy Galleria is unhappy with the way her life is going. Her life plans were to be married, excelling in her career, and pregnant with her first child. However, her boyfriend, Phil, has other plans. Trying to make partner at his law firm, his plans don't include a family, marriage or setting roots anytime soon. Happy has always been good with remaining emotionless, but will her emotions start to show once Phil ignores her pleas for wanting more in their relationship?

While rushing to her gate for her birthday trip to Bora Bora that her sister surprised her with, Happy bumps into a man – literally. Peeved that the man has delayed her from making her flight, she yells, curses and continues to her gate.

That man is her pilot. Colt Wright is a pilot who has worked himself from the ground up and has just moved his family from New York to Atlanta to work with a top airline. A single father to a ten-year-old girl, and trying to keep his eye on his aging mother, Colt Wright doesn't have time for small talk. After losing his child's mother to cancer, he wants more than casual talk or one night stands. He wants a woman – the Wright woman.

These two cross paths and nothing may remain the same. Happy has baggage, but Colt is used to dealing with baggage, being a pilot and all. *Will Happy remain Emotionless?*

Chapter One

FIRST COMES CAREER, THEN COMES RING?

Happy

Tonight is the night, he's going to do it, I coached myself as I walked into Benihana for my birthday dinner. I had spent the entire day working and thinking of my birthday dinner that my boyfriend, Phil, told me he was throwing me. At first, I thought it was odd that he didn't make it a surprise theme, then I automatically thought of him popping the question. My parents, his parents, and my sisters were going to be there. He invited them all, so I knew he was going to pop the question. All day, I couldn't focus on the pile of work and emails I had because I was waiting for tonight. My mind wandered to what kind of ring he had bought, how he would get on one knee and what words he would choose to sweep me off my feet? Phil was a man of very few words, however, the few words he said always had special meaning to them.

As soon as the time hit, I rushed out of my home office and jumped right into my car to speed to Alpharetta where the restaurant was located. My sister, Kharisma, had already called a bunch of times to remind me that I was running late. We had lived here our entire lives and I still couldn't get used to the Atlanta traffic. There was no rhyme or reason for the traffic. When my black Fendi booties crossed the threshold of the restaurant, I saw my sister, parents, and Phil with his parents, waiting. I knew he was going to do it. My hands were shaking before we even got seated. I walked in and greeted everyone, then kissed my man on the lips.

"The traffic getting here was terrible," I complained.

"It's your day, we're fine with waiting on you." My mother was the first to speak as she walked over and kissed me on the forehead.

"Thank you, Mommy."

"Happy Birthday, Happy Patty." My father, Paul, pulled me into a huge bear hug. My mother always told the story of how he had called me that since they'd decided my name would be Happy.

"Jade couldn't make it. You know Tony has that deal overseas, so she went to be with him," she informed me of my oldest sister's recent moves.

Jade was engaged to one of the top real estate agents in the state of Georgia. We had known the Blatimore family for years. It was an ongoing joke that our parents had arranged their marriage since they were children. However, Jade was always running behind Tony and I could count on one hand how many times she had actually shown up for me like she did for her man.

"Fix your face, baby girl. I'm here, so that counts way more than Jade." My father tried to brighten up my mood. For once, it would have been nice for my sister to show up to something that had something to do with me.

"Thanks, Daddy. I do appreciate you being here. When do you fly out?" I raised my eyebrow because I knew he would be going out of town soon.

My father was an entrepreneur, but his most prized possession was our chain of stores, Galleria Co. My father started it from the ground up when he was in his twenties. He started the business with three hundred dollars and his word. Today, it was worth millions and one of the best department stores in Atlanta. Our family was royalty in Atlanta. However, I was trying to get my father to open some stores in other states, but you couldn't teach an old dog new tricks.

"You don't need to worry." He kissed me on the forehead. Phil walked over to both of us and kissed me on the cheek.

"Honey, you didn't need to drive into work this morning. I would have picked you up on my way from the office," Phil informed me.

Phil was a lawyer, and a good one, too. He was one of the top defense attorneys in Atlanta. We had been together for four years and we still didn't live together. I was his girlfriend, and he made the world aware of that, but often, I felt like his shiny toy in his trophy shelf. He invited me to all the important dinners, galas and parties, but I was still his girlfriend after four years. Tonight, that was going to change. I was going to become his fiancée, plan our wedding, and move into a beautiful home here in Alpharetta, where we would begin working on making a baby. My plans and Phil's plans were the complete opposite. He was consumed with work, climbing up the cooperate ladder more, and making partner at his firm. I understood all that he wanted, however, I wanted to know when settling down and starting a family would come into play?

Today was my twenty-ninth birthday and I wasn't married, I didn't have a child, and I still had a boyfriend. My parents wanted grandchildren yesterday and I couldn't tell them I was at least close to completing the goal of getting pregnant. Phil and I didn't even live together, although I had tried to make it happen. I told him plenty of times that he could move in with me, or I would move in with him. When I closed on my townhome a few months ago, I asked him about us moving in together. He brushed it off and surprised me with a Chanel bag a few days later. Like I usually did, I pushed the situation to the backburner and decided to leave it alone for now.

"It was fine. I didn't want you coming from Midtown to Buckhead." I smiled and placed my hand in his.

We were all seated about the table and I smiled, looking at everyone I loved gathered around the table. Phil acted like what I had said went in one ear and right out the other, but he had been listening and I couldn't believe I was going to be an engaged woman at the end of the night. Kharisma smiled at me as she sat with her legs crossed.

Phil kissed me on the forehead as we sat down and placed our order. The chef came out, introduced himself and got right to cooking. He saw we were all chatting, so he didn't bother trying to entertain us as he prepared our meal.

"How's your stylist thing going, Happy?" Kendra, Phil's mother, asked me.

I quit my job as the stylist who put together all the shoots and campaigns for my father's company. I wasn't happy and I had to follow my father's direction. The money was wonderful, still, I wasn't happy because I couldn't express myself creatively. I was working under my father and then a senior stylist who was in her sixties. I tried to get my father to see things my way and brighten up the company. Even after my pitch, he turned me down and told me he was staying true to the Galleria way, which was boring. My happiness was being drained from me every time I stepped into her office downtown, so I sent my father an email and resigned and started doing freelance work. It had been six months since I quit working for my father and work was slow, yet it was still progressing.

"I actually have a few meetings lined up with some of the celebrities on *Love & Hip Hop: Atlanta*."

"That's amazing. And how's the blog doing? I was waiting on my email notification to go off last night," she laughed.

I had a fashion blog called Happy G that had over a million subscribers. They lived for my outfit of the day blogs or my reviews on what I thought of new fashion pieces that released. I loved writing on my blog and helping other aspiring stylists find their way. It made me happy to write and give my honest opinion on fashion pieces. The thing was, I didn't want to be behind my desk writing blogs. I wanted to be behind curtains, getting models together and styling them, or helping a rich wife who had nothing to do other than pay me to put fly outfits together for her and her kids.

"It's going great. I forgot to put my post up because I was on the phone with Phil half the night."

"You both are meant to be together. I told Phil he picked a winner. When you were late meeting me because you had a meeting, I knew you were the one. He needs a woman that's built like he is, business-minded." She smiled and touched her husband's hand.

"Happy gets that from her father. This man will work until the day he dies," my mother added. "I'm so proud of her and everything she's doing. Now, if only she gives me some grandbabies," she made sure to mention like she mentioned every time we got on the phone.

"Ah, come on, parents... no baby talk." Kharisma switched the subject. "I want to say a toast for Happy." She smiled and raised her champagne flute. "Hap, you know I love you and admire how hard you work. When you quit working with Dad, I thought you were crazy," she laughed. "You were crazy. You were crazy, determined and destined to rise, on your own terms, which you have. Everything we spoke about as kids is coming to fruition for you, and I couldn't be more proud of you. I love you, Hap, and I can't wait to board the plane in two days to Bora Bora." She raised her glass and I wiped away a tear.

Fashion had been my life since I was a child. I loved everything about clothes from the look and feel of it, to how it looked when you put it together. It was only right that I went to work for my father and gain some experience. I thought I had the perfect job and, at first, I could admit I did. I was the boss' daughter and everyone automatically wanted to please me. My father wanted to keep me on a short string and he always reminded me that Galleria was his name first and this company was his. I couldn't be free in my position, and the more years I spent there, the more unhappy I became. I was craving to bust out of there and show the world what Happy Galleria could pull and put together. My father supported me and loved me, but in the end, he knew he had to let me sink or swim. Luckily, I had enough savings where I was swimming and I had some great clients who weren't cheap. I knew I wanted more and that with hard work, I was going to continue to bust my ass until I was a known stylist in the fashion industry. It was going to take me that much longer because I didn't want to use my last name. It was the main reason I had started my blog three years ago as Happy G. I didn't want to use my father, his name or his brand to build myself up. When it was all said and done, I wanted to say that I got where I was because of me.

"I love you, Kharisma." I blew a kiss at her. "I appreciate everything you've done for me." It was no secret that Kharisma and I were sisters and best friends. Out of both of my sisters, she was who I went to the most when I needed to chat. With me just turning twenty-nine and her being thirty, it was apparent why we were so close. Our older sister, Jade, was thirty-three, and she always felt out of the loop when we did sister dates.

Everyone chatted about everyday things as we ate our food. The chef had wished me a happy birthday before he cleaned his station and excused himself. I was enjoying my favorite meal here, seafood delight, as I looked at Phil every few seconds. He was talking with my mother and she was asking him about work and his future.

"Of course your daughter is in my future. You don't understand how happy she makes me." He kissed me on the cheek as I took a bite of my calamari.

"I love you, baby," I told him.

"I want to say a toast and give my baby her gift. I know she's been waiting all night for it, so I want to give it to her before she melts in anticipation," he chuckled and stood up.

Food was the last thing on my mind. I was about to get proposed to and I couldn't have food stuck in my cheek or teeth when he popped the question. Even my mother stopped eating because I had been talking to her about it for weeks. Phil asked me randomly what kind of ring I wanted when he got ready to pop the question and that was all I needed to know.

"Baby, you know I love the hell out of you. I love how hard you work and how hard you allow me to work. You don't complain when I can't make a date night and I appreciate you for that. I want to ask you one question and I hope you'll say yes," he started. "Will you move in with me?"

"Yes, baby, yes!" I jumped up and screamed loudly with tears threatening to come down my eyes. "I'll marry you!"

Phil looked at me confused and everyone else stared on as well. "Baby, I asked would you move in with me," he clarified, and I was mortified. He had said it so fast, I heard what I wanted to hear. Then, he held a small velvet box in his hands and I assumed that was my ring.

"You what?"

"Doll, I asked you to move in with me. I know it's something you asked about a few months ago and I brushed it off, but I'm ready to wake up to your beautiful face every morning instead of just the weekend." He gently brushed the side of my face, then opened the box and there stood a gold key on a Tiffany's keychain.

Phil lived in a high rise in Midtown. It was beautiful and up so high, everyone below looked like ants. The one thing I hated was the traffic that surrounded his condo. When you stepped out onto his balcony, you heard the hustle and bustle of the city. It was nowhere near New York's midtown, but it was still noisy, and I loved the quiet. I lived in a townhouse in a gated community in Buckhead. I loved that I could sit on my balcony and sip tea without hearing a bunch of horns blowing or people chatting loudly. As much as I wanted to live with Phil, I had become so accustomed to my townhouse I had bought and loved it.

"I.. I thought you were proposing..." I allowed my voice to trail off. Here I stood, in the middle of this restaurant, mortified that the question he asked wasn't the question I thought he asked.

"Babe, we spoke about this," he hugged me and whispered in my ear.

With my parents and his parents here, I knew not to press the issue. I decided to smile and make a light joke and continue to try to enjoy the rest of my dinner. I didn't understand why he invited everyone when we could have just had dinner with the both of us. The rest of dinner floated by because I didn't pay attention to anything that was going on.

"Babe, we spoke about the engagement thing. I thought we were clear that I'm not ready to take that step," Phil brought up as he walked me over to my car.

"And I thought I told you I'm not going to be a girlfriend for much longer. I'm twenty-nine years old, Phil. You're ready to shack up, but not give me a commitment?"

"Hap, you're acting like it will never happen. I'm just saying I'm worried about making partner right now. An engagement and a wedding isn't what I need right now."

"Well, I don't know if this relationship is what I need right now. I'm twenty-nine and I don't want to be a girlfriend forever. It's not like I'm asking to walk down the aisle tomorrow. I want to be someone's wife. You don't think it hurts when someone asks when you're finally going to marry me or when we're going to have children?"

"You just quit your job six months ago, Happy. You're still trying to make whatever you're doing work. Stop letting people force you into things. We're moving on our own time." He kissed me on the lips. "Happy birthday, baby. I would come over, but I have to get up early for court in the morning. I'll try to come by tomorrow so I can see you before you leave for your trip with

Kharisma." He hugged me and I looked at him through saddened eyes.

What did he mean I was still trying to make whatever I was doing work? What I was doing wasn't whatever, it was a career. When I told Phil I quit my job, he wasn't excited. In fact, he told me I needed to go beg my father for my job back. The only thing that eased his mind was the fact that he knew I still had a trust fund to live off of. When I told him I quit my job, and the reason, he laughed. He told me it was a stupid reason, and that if I wanted to be free, I might as well live off my father's money instead of trying to work for it. It was things like that that made me dislike Phil at times. Then, he ended up doing something that caused me to smile and want to marry him.

After he closed my car door, I started my car and headed to Walmart and grabbed two bottles of wine, ice cream, and pretzels. Tonight was my birthday, and I was bringing it in with wine, ice cream, and some pretzels. Happy birthday to me.

§

"You mean to tell me you didn't get no dick last night? It was your birthday, everyone gets dick on their birthday." Kharisma sipped her Frappuccino and looked at me, puzzled.

"I barely got the kiss he offered. Claimed he's going to make it up to me when we're back from our vacation."

Kharisma rolled her eyes. "I'm sorry you didn't get any dick last night. What exactly did you do?" She squinted her eyes and looked at me as she twirled her tongue around the red straw.

"I grabbed some wine and ice cream from Walmart," I sighed. It sounded pathetic when I said it out loud. Last night, I cracked open a bottle of wine, grabbed a spoon and brought the ice cream into my bed while I binge watched old episodes of *Sex and the City*. Where was my Mr. Biggs?

"Wow, Happy. The old you would have called up one of your exes. Where's the old Hap at?" Kharisma laughed loudly.

We were at our favorite coffee shop, close to Lennox Square. Once we were done, we planned to run and get some last minute things for our trip, then end the day with some lunch. Tomorrow we would be sitting in business class on our way to Bora Bora. As much as I fought my sister on her choice of a birthday gift for me, I knew I needed to take time away from working and Phil. Bora Bora was the last place on my list to visit, but it was probably needed to get my mind right and come home with a fresh outlook.

"I didn't need the headache. Plus, I can't do that to Phil. I'm actually in a relationship and can't cheat on him."

"You can't or you won't?"

"What is your deal with me cheating on my boyfriend?"

"Don't get me wrong, Phil is amazing on paper. If I saw everything about him written down on paper, I would be impressed and would probably be ready to hand over my panties to him. However, I've met Phil and the personal side of him sucks. He doesn't want to be committed, he still lives like he's a bachelor, and all he does is work. Let's not mention he disregards your feelings and career choice. Hap, he literally thinks you sit home and play with clothes all day. His respect for your career is the biggest turn off about him. It amazes me that you even tolerate him since your career means the world to you." She took a sip from her drink. "And, the only reason he gave you a key to his place is because you mentioned it months prior and he figured he could shut you up with the key to his place instead of actually producing a ring."

Kharisma was a pediatrician and owned her own practice. It took her a while, but she stepped out on faith two years ago and decided to open her own. I was so proud because my sister worked herself up and had managed to obtain some celebrity patients. She couldn't talk about them, but she made sure to mention she had a few celebrity children she cared for in her practice. Kharisma Kids was a very kid friendly practice and that was what she wanted when she designed it. She wanted a doctor's office that didn't intimidate children when they had to go to the doctor. Just like she did with her patients' parents, she gave it to me straight. She didn't hold back on her advice and opinions and I didn't expect her to.

"Maybe he's right. Getting married and everything before he makes partner would be too much. Plus, I'm really not where I want to be in my career, either. I have clients, but not as many as I want."

"You're now making excuses for him," she called me out. "You're twenty-nine and have been wanting to be married forever. You've wasted four years and you both are nowhere near building a future. So, don't try and convince me you're satisfied with this." She pursed her lips like she did when she was calling me out on my bullshit.

"Khar, I don't want to waste another four years of my life to start over with someone else. I'm being a brat and expecting it because I want it now." I was doing exactly what she was calling me out for.

"Hap, you know what you're doing. Right now, we don't need to get too deep into it. If and when you're ready to end things with Phil, you will."

Why did she automatically assume I was going to be done with Phil? I sipped my coffee and tried to picture myself laying on a beach for a full week without work, Phil, or having to sort out my future. I wanted to relax and regroup so when I touched back down in Atlanta, I was ready to deal with whatever I needed to deal with.

Chapter Two

SHE MIGHT BE THE WRIGHT ONE

Colt

I handed my badge over as I bypassed the long security lines at TSA with my phone glued to my ear. Hartsfield International Airport was always crowded. The lines were always wrapped around the corner and the staff was overworked. Thankfully, I breezed through the airport like a celebrity and didn't have to wait long to get through the lines. I pulled my luggage behind me and continued to head to my terminal. I was already running late and had ten minutes to be across the airport for my flight.

"Watch it, fool!" I heard a woman squeal as we crashed right into each other. I wasn't paying attention, and she had to be doing the same because we collided into each other coming from two different directions. "I'm going to be late for my flight because you don't know how to watch where you're going!" she continued to holler as she gathered her Gucci purse and Louis Vuitton luggage off the floor.

"I mean, who the fool? You bumped into me, too," I replied.

"Whatever! Just watch where you're going!" she scolded over

her shoulder as she took off the same way I was heading. She wore six-inch pumps and tried to juggle walking on her heels, rolling her luggage and texting whoever she was adamant about texting during her trek through the airport.

"Colt, you there?"

"Yeah, I'm sorry, mama. Some lady just bumped into me," I apologized to my mother, who I had forgotten I was on the phone with previous to bumping into the woman. "How is she doing?"

"Colt, you just left the house not too long ago," she laughed. "River is going to be fine, and I know how to break that stubborn fever. Remember, I raised you." She took the chance to remind me of something I already knew.

"Mama, I don't like leaving town when she's not feeling good. River never misses school, and then I'm going to be away for a few days."

"You've planned this trip for three months. You're an amazing father, but every parent needs their time. I have her under control, and I bet when you land, she'll be all better."

"I hope so." I sighed as I approached my gate.

"She will be. Safe travels, baby. We love you and will send up a prayer for you," she told me as we ended the call.

My mother was the rock in our family. She was what kept me grounded and allowed me to live my life and pursue my career. If it wasn't for her, I wouldn't have been able to do what I do now. River was ten years old and the spitting image of her mother. She was such a girly girl and I didn't know how the fuck I was supposed to handle that. My little baby girl was into clothes, nails and having her hair pressed straight. How the hell was I supposed to handle all that? All those damn baby books, I never came across them growing up into little women.

"Man, I just knew you were going to miss this plane and I was going to have to fly," Darrius, my co-pilot, laughed.

"River is sick, so I was considering taking off," I explained and put my luggage in the cockpit.

"Damn, my little princess needs to get better. She's supposed to come over next week to hang with Savannah," he reminded me.

"Yeah, Mama saying she gonna get that cold up out of her." I laughed and sat in the cockpit.

"If anybody can get that cold up out of her, it's your mama," he laughed and patted me on the shoulder as he went to greet the passengers boarding the plane.

Flying had been something I'd been obsessed with since I was a child. I always wanted to know how something so big and metal could take flight and fly to another part of the world. I went to college, flight school and did all the training I needed to become a pilot. I busted my ass to get where I needed to be and didn't make any excuses. At thirty-three, I was living my life on my terms and was happy with my career choice. I had traveled to so many different countries in the world and did it while working. I found peace flying above the clouds. A year ago, I got tired of working for my other job and decided to apply to Delta. I flew to their home base here in Atlanta and aced the interview. It wasn't even three hours after the interview and they sent me a contract to negotiate a salary. With how much flying experience I had under my belt, they had to pay me well in order to keep me.

The only issue was that my base was in Atlanta. I could catch a two and half hour flight from New York on my days I worked, or I could move. Moving my baby girl was the hardest thing I had to do, but I was doing this for her future. My mother packed up her life to come along and make sure that River was grounded with me traveling often. We moved to Lawrenceville, Georgia. It was a suburb of Atlanta and away from the hustle of the city. Gwinnett County was one of the best school districts in the state, so it was an easy choice right off the back. Coming from Brooklyn, New York, it took a while for us to become adjusted. We were both born and raised in the city, so the city was all we knew. I was born and raised in Brownsville, Brooklyn. Half my friends I grew up with were dead or locked up.

Going away to college was what saved me. If I didn't have a

praying mother, I didn't know where I would be right now. My mother was always there with her bible, prayer cloth and a good word to keep me grounded and on the right path. My father was somewhere out there being a rolling stone, and I wasn't mad at him. He missed out on raising me and I gave all the credit to my mother. Black women didn't get the credit they deserved. They were prayer warriors, nurses, therapist and everything wrapped up in one. I wasn't ashamed to say I wanted a woman just like my mother. I wanted a woman who, when times got hard, she got down on her knees and prayed with me, not turned the other way and ran.

"Captain, we're all boarded," Cynthia, one of the flight attendants, came out and told me. With every flight, I liked to come out and greet the passengers. Wasn't nothing scarier than not knowing who was flying your plane.

Love you both. I sent my mother a text message before I powered my phone off and went to speak to the passengers.

As soon as I got to the front, I saw the woman I bumped into. She was sitting in business class with her legs crossed, a water bottle, and was chatting with a light-skinned woman sitting beside her. When she looked up, she rolled her eyes and nudged her friend. I knew she was probably talking about me, so I smirked.

"Good morning, everyone. I'm your captain. Today's flight should be nice and easy with little to no turbulence. The weather in California is around eighty degrees, so it's a nice break from the cold we're getting here in Atlanta. Make sure to keep your seat belts on, even if the seatbelt sign is off. Sit back, relax, and I'll get us up in the air and to our destination on time." I made sure to look directly at the woman and winked.

"Girl, he's fine. I wouldn't be mad if I bumped right into him," her friend said loud enough for me to hear. The woman put her hand over her face looking mortified. I chuckled and went into the cockpit. The first officer locked the door and I sat down behind the controls and bent my head down in prayer. It was never easy flying this plane. I had all these passengers' lives in my hand. They depended on me to lift them up thirty thousand feet in the air, and then bring them back down so they could reunite with their families. It was me who would be blamed if this shit went wrong, so I never took it for granted.

"So, man, you excited for your vacation? You haven't taken off since you moved here," Darrius made sure to mention.

"Yeah, I'm just worried about my seed, you know?"

"Nah, I know for sure. She's gonna be good. I'll be sure to check in on her and your mama while you're gone."

"Appreciate it, man," I thanked him as I flipped all the switches and started navigating toward the take-off strip.

"No problem. You know y'all family." Darrius and his family had welcomed me and my family as soon as we moved here. He was from upstate New York and had moved his family here, too. We bonded on the fact that we were from New York and living in Georgia.

"What's the history with you and shorty?"

"Ah, you caught that?"

"Man, I peep everything," he laughed. "What's up with her?"

"She bumped into me earlier. Nothing more and nothing less," I explained.

"Uh-huh. Man, you need to get out there and date. Since you've been here, I haven't seen you go out on one date. All you do is work, and when you're not working, you're tied into River's life."

"Man, she got mad shit going on with all the school teams she's a part of."

"Yeah, but what is left for you when she goes to bed at night? Even your mama is dating," he continued to clown me.

"I'm not in my mama's business like that, and she's not in mine, either."

"Well, I'm in both of y'all business and you need to get some business," he continued as I tuned him out while I prepared to take off.

I didn't date because women were more of a headache. Half of them couldn't understand that I had responsibilities other than kissing their ass. I had a family to support and couldn't afford to be chasing them around or playing kid games. I needed a real-ass woman who knew she would be treated like a queen, as long as she allowed me to take care of business.

"Well, I will say that I'm glad you're going on vacation. Man, Bora Bora, you go big, huh?"

"It's been three years since I took a vacation." I had planned this vacation months ago and it was finally happening. I was flying to California, then I had a layover to board my next flight that was going to take me there. I figured I might as well get some work in while I was on my way to vacation in Bora Bora for the next week and a half.

"Yeah, you deserve every bit. Don't go calling your mama and River every five minutes," he clowned and I shook my head and pulled down the lever as the plane took off up into the sky. *Godspeed*, I said to myself like I did with every flight.

§

I sat down in business class and pulled out my iPad and headphones. The perk of being a pilot was that I was able to snag seats for half the price, and sometimes, they were free. The bungalow I was staying at in my hotel cost me more than flying there. It was a trip I had always wanted to take with my daughter's mother, Tamia. We had planned to go here, but life got in the way and that never happened.

"Girl, I can't believe we have to sit across from each other. This airline is really starting to piss me off." The woman I bumped into plopped down beside me. She was so busy talking to her friend, she didn't notice I was sitting beside her. "And, I requested a window seat last week," she continued to complain.

Her friend noticed me and smirked at me as she looked back to her friend. "Happy, this is your birthday trip. You need to stop complaining and take in the moment and the view."

"View? What view do I have sitting in the aisle seat?"

"Oh, you'll see." She pulled her headphones on, crossed her legs, and opened one of the few magazines she had sitting in her purse next to her feet.

"And she's ignoring me. I can't believe this." She finally leaned back in the chair and strapped her seatbelt. It was then when she looked over and noticed me. "Great. As if this flight couldn't get any better."

"I don't mind giving up my window seat," I offered.

"No, I'm fine," she smugly replied and reached down and dug into her purse. She pulled out a Louis Vuitton planner, laptop and headphones.

The flight took off and I leaned back with my headphones as I admired the beauty she was. She had light brown skin that looked like honey when the sun hit it at the right moment. Her golden brown curls hung wildly. She continued to push a few out of her face whenever they fell onto her forehead. Even with a frown on her face, you could tell when she smiled, she could light up an entire room. To her pointy nose, down to the set of juicy lips God had blessed her with were all beautiful features on this queen. She placed a pair of prescription glasses on the bridge of her nose and spoke to herself occasionally as she wrote things down in her planner. She had to be no more than 5'5 and weighed no more than a hundred and fifty pounds, but that didn't include those bumble bee stings that sat on her front and the back. Queen had a nice body on her and I could tell it was homegrown, not that mess women bought from their doctors.

"My name is Colt Wright." I took my headphones out and extended my hand.

"Why would I need or want to know your name?" she snapped back and continued to tap away at her computer.

"I mean, we're going to be on this flight for seven hours. I figured we might as well become acquainted."

"We're sitting on this plane and then we'll never see each other ever again," she snapped and continued working on her computer. I placed my headphones back in my ear and looked out the window. I was trying to be nice to shorty and she was being snappy. Shit, I had bigger things on my mind to think about, like my daughter.

I felt her gently tap me and I took one of my headphones out of my ear. "I'm sorry for being so rude. I've had a rough week, you know," she apologized and offered a smile. I could see the dimples that her scowl had been hiding. "I almost missed my flight this morning and I'm taking all my problems out on you. I wanted to thank you for getting us from Atlanta to California safely."

"You're very welcome. I'm having a hard week, too. My daughter is sick and I'm going on vacation," I sighed.

"Oh no, how old is she?"

"She's ten."

"I'm sorry. I've been being a bitch and you're worried about your daughter."

"Nah, you good. My mother has her, but I'm a dad, so I worry."

"Parents need time away, too. I'm not a parent yet, but my mother always took vacations without me or my sisters."

"Thanks. I'm trying to get used to this vacation thing."

"I'm never good at going on vacation. I bring my laptop and end up working the entire time." She offered me another smile. "Like now, I'm working on my schedule once I'm back home and I haven't even arrived at the resort yet."

"Yeah, I'm a bit of a workaholic, too."

"I don't want to talk your ear off, so I'll get back to my work schedule," she smiled. "Oh, and if you're ever looking for a stylist for you or your daughter, give me a call." She reached into her planner and handed me a gold foil business card.

"Happy Galleria," I read out loud. "You work in Galleria's? I buy my daughter's clothes from there."

"I've been so busy working I haven't updated my cards. I used to work there, but I quit a couple months ago. If you ever need your daughter styled for an event, or need someone to pull some clothes for her, give me a call."

"Quit? I drive by the main store almost every morning. I heard there is a waiting list just to work in those stores. The benefits are good, too, I heard."

"My father knows how to treat his employees, just not his family," she mumbled and didn't think I heard.

"So, you're an infamous Galleria?" I chuckled. Darrius had gotten offered a chance to fly the Galleria's family jet to London, but turned down the offer. That family was pretty top notch, and everyone who was anyone knew who the Galleria family was.

"I like to go as Happy. I don't like to throw my last name around." She blushed and looked down at her planner.

"How does one get a name like Happy?"

"My mother said I was always bouncing around in her stomach, so she knew I was Happy. Plus, I was the last girl and she was happy she didn't have a boy." She smiled as she explained how she had gotten her name.

"Good to know." I nodded and placed her card in the back of my iPad case. Laying my head back on the headrest, I put my headphone back in my ear and continued to look out the window. Eventually, my tired body won and I drifted off to sleep.

Chapter Three

WELCOME TO PARADISE

Happy

Bora Bora was absolutely beautiful. We were staying at the Four Seasons and it was more beautiful than any picture I had ever seen. For the first three days, we lounged around and drank until we were both too drunk to make it back to our bungalows on the water. This was exactly what we both needed. Me and my sister sitting on an island together, sharing cocktails and conversations. Not once did I think about Phil, the engagement I should have had, or anything that happened last week. Kharisma made sure I didn't think of any of those things as she continued to hand me shots of the rum the resort was known for. Kharisma had been so bogged down with work, this was a getaway for her, too, so I understood why she wanted to let loose and let her hair down.

Today, I grabbed my book and decided to sit on the beach and watch the sunset. Kharisma was hungover in her bungalow, recovering from the night before. I spent the entire day puking and grabbing the side of my toilet that by the time five o'clock hit, I was tired of being cooped up in my bungalow. After showering and knocking on my sister's bungalow, I found myself sitting at the beach bar with a buffalo chicken sandwich and French fries while sucking down a club soda to settle my queasy stomach. It was so weird that my stomach was queasy, yet I was as hungry as a hostage. I stuffed some fries into my mouth and opened my Kindle to catch up on a book.

"Damn, you fucking them fries up," I heard a familiar deep voice come up behind me. Drinking my club soda, I gulped down the food that was in my mouth and looked up. It was Colt. Once we landed, Kharisma and I went our way and he went his own way. There were plenty of other resorts on the island, so I assumed he had stayed at one of those.

"Hey... you," I greeted him and flipped my kindle case closed. "I didn't know you were staying on this resort." I turned and watched as he settled in the bar stool beside me.

"You didn't ask."

"Now, why would I ask you where you're staying? That would have been weird." I giggled and popped another fry into my mouth.

"From a beautiful woman like you... I wouldn't have taken it as weird."

"Why, thank you. How is your daughter doing?"

"Ah, you remembered," he smiled.

This man walked, talked and carried himself like the fine specimen he was. His brown skin glistened as beads of perspiration accumulated on his forehead. How you made sweating look sexy, I didn't know, but he somehow had mastered it. His dark-brown bedroom eyes looked right into your soul when he looked at you. I watched as he swiped his nose, and when Beyoncé said Jackson Five nostrils, I felt that because his nose was a work of art. Then, when you got down to his lips, they were juicy and I could imagine the things he could do with lips so big and juicy. His beard was thick, still cut short and groomed. He stood around 6'3 with a muscular build. I could tell he worked out and probably enjoyed it. He sat in front of me shirtless and I wanted to use my index finger to trace every vein, muscle and six pac he had. He spoke with an accent, and I couldn't quite catch where he was from. I knew one thing; he wasn't from Atlanta.

"I did. Is she better? Want?" I offered some of my food and he declined with a bright smile on his face.

"Nah, I'm good. She's doing much better. My mother got her better, but she has a bit of a cough, which I'll take."

"Good, I'm glad she's better."

"You and your friend always get lit like that?" he chuckled, and I was sure my cheeks turned red from embarrassment. Kharisma and I had gotten so drunk the night before on the beach. The workers continued to bring us drinks and we didn't stop until we had to be escorted to our bungalows.

"You saw that, huh?"

"I did. Was walking past from dinner and wanted to join, but y'all were well past lit and decided to turn in for the night early."

"She's my sister, by the way. This trip has been a long time coming. We've both been so stressed." I took another bite out of my sandwich. "You sure you don't want some?"

"Ma, I'm good. I just had something to eat not too long ago from the swim-up bar."

"How is it over there? We've been over here at this bar since we came. I haven't tried any of the restaurants here. I've kinda been living off these buffalo chicken sandwiches."

"Damn, you don't know what you missing. I been eating lobster almost every night." I wondered what his salary looked like. This resort wasn't all-inclusive, so how much did he make to afford lobster every night?

"If I can drag my sister out of bed tonight, I'll have to try one out."

"Let me take you to one of the restaurants," he suggested.

I smiled and shook my head no. "I don't think my boyfriend would like that too much." Sitting in front of a fine man like Colt, it was easy for a girl to forget she had a boyfriend back home. I wasn't the type of woman who had one-night stands, however, with

Colt, if I was single, I just might have taken that chance to see how he worked in bed.

"I didn't ask to go out with you or marry you. Dinner. An innocent dinner, and I'm alone."

"Why did you come here alone? No girlfriend or friends?"

"No woman worth spending this type of money on, and my friends have jobs and families. They can't afford to pick up and come to Bora Bora for two weeks."

"You're brave to travel here all alone. I don't think I would be able to do it."

"I'm gonna die alone."

"Not true. You can die in a plane crash, that wouldn't be alone." It was a dark joke and I often made dark jokes that no one understood. He surprised me when he laughed at my twisted sense of humor.

"You're right. Maybe I could find an older lady to nestle next to and die in her breasts," he added onto the joke.

"Only if she hasn't stashed all of the mini bottles of liquors in her breasts. It might be a bit hard for you to get comfortable during your last moments." I busted out laughing right along with him.

"Nah, you corny," he continued to laugh.

"You're laughing, though," I made sure to point out. "My mother hates when I'm dark with my jokes."

"Yeah, older people tend to not think the same way we do. My mom hates when I make plane jokes since I'm a pilot," he smirked. "Now, about that dinner?"

I sat there chewing on my piece of fry and thought about what he was asking. Dinner was harmless. Phil went out to dinner with plenty of female colleagues and I didn't complain.

"I'll tell you what... Let me check on my sister and see what she says, and if she's still not up to it, you can come to my bungalow around ten. I'm in bungalow twelve."

"Bet. I gotta be honest, I'm kinda hoping your sister still fucked up." I laughed so loud, I snorted. "I see why your mama named you Happy. That damn smile is beautiful," he winked and got up from the stool.

I knew I was sitting up on this bar stool grinning like a teenage girl at a prom. "Thank you. See you in a bit," I replied and he gently grabbed my hand. A volt of electric shock flowed through my body as his big hands swallowed my petite ones up. He gave my hand a gentle squeeze, then smiled before turning to head in the opposite direction.

I quickly gobbled down the rest of my food, left a tip for the bartender and quickly headed back to our bungalows. Since Kharisma wasn't feeling well, I made sure to swipe her keycard so I could get back into her bungalow. Lightly tapping, I peeked my head in before I squeezed through the small opening and closed it behind me. Right where I had left her before, she was sprawled out on her bed with pillows over her head.

"Khar, wake up!" I pulled her blankets off her legs, then went to open her shades. The sun was setting, but it was still light outside.

"Happy, take your ass out of my room, please. I'm tired and feel like I'm going to vomit the more I try to sit up," she whispered harshly and pulled the covers back over her body.

"Remember the guy from the plane?"

"The pilot you were being evil to?" she shot back from under her cover.

"I wasn't being evil. I eventually apologized and we spoke for a few. You would have known if you didn't take a damn sleeping pill."

"Flying isn't my thing, Happy. Sleeping pills help me cope with flying. You didn't tell me you guys spoke." She finally pulled her head up from under the blanket.

"It wasn't important." I waved her off because this wasn't what I wanted to tell her. "Well, he's staying on the resort and wants to take me to dinner."

Kharisma was on her deathbed four seconds ago, but as soon as the words left my mouth, she whipped those covers off her body and stared at me with wide eyes. "And you better had told him you would."

"I didn't tell him no. I just told him I had to check with you and make sure you didn't want to grab anything to eat together."

While I spoke, she slipped her toes into her Versace slides and grabbed my hand to pull me out the door. She paused briefly at how bright the sun was when she opened the door, then continued right across the walkway to my bungalow.

"What are you doing?" I laughed as she pulled me inside and shut the door behind her.

"Uh, you're going to dinner with that fine-ass man. I've never seen a black pilot in my life as fine as he is."

"Kharisma Galleria, you tend to forget I have a boyfriend," I reminded her like I did every time a cute man decided to flirt with me.

Kharisma loved to forget that I had a boyfriend and that I was actively pursuing an engagement from him. "And you tend to forget I don't care. You need to go and have dinner with him. You never know, you may have some fun."

I plopped down on the couch and watched as she looked through my luggage for an outfit. Usually, I would unpack my things and get comfortable, but I had been too drunk to do anything these past few days.

"Kharisma, me going out with him is basically cheating. You didn't see how he held my hand and looked into my eyes."

She turned around and gasped so loud, I thought something happened to her. "You didn't tell me all of that."

"It happened so fast, I forgot to mention it."

"Happy, you're on vacation miles and miles away from Phil. I'm not saying you should have sex with the man, but you should definitely go out to dinner with him. After everything that happened with Phil for your birthday, you need to keep your options open. Remember, you're twenty-nine," she tossed in my age and I sighed.

I knew I wanted more and Phil just wanted to make partner. Having children, getting married and all the things I wanted weren't things he was interested in. I knew making partner was his focus and he had promised that after he made partner, he was going to do and be everything I wanted. His firm was working him hard and Phil took every case they handed him. We barely had time together because when he wasn't working, he was home working on a case. Even on date nights, Phil would be so consumed with trying to explain a case to me. Being a wife of a lawyer was something I was prepared to be because I had sacrificed so much in our relationship already. My fear was ending things and having to start over with someone else. What if that person didn't want marriage or children and I had ended it with Phil, who could possibly end up giving me what I'd been asking for. I had to be patient and I realized I had no other choice but to be.

Growing up, I was used to getting every and anything I wanted, when I wanted it. My parents gave me and my sisters whatever we wanted. It sucked when you became an adult and realized you couldn't have everything right when you wanted it. If it was up to me, I would have been married and expecting my second baby already. Except, I was twenty-nine without any children and begging for an engagement.

"Even if me and Phil were on a break, I'm not looking for anything new right now. He's a nice man and very handsome. Still, I don't want to deal with that right now."

"Deal with what? You don't want to deal with that, but you're willing to deal with a dead-end relationship?"

"You're acting like you and Tommi are so perfect."

"We're not discussing me and my relationship right now. We're focused on you and this date." She held up the dress she had picked. Kharisma picked out a strapless, fuchsia pink, flowy maxi dress, a pair of Dolce & Gabbana wedges with the matching clutch. "Thank God you're a stylist because everything is basically paired up."

"You don't think I'd be doing too much?" I wondered.

"You go from not wanting to go to asking if you're doing too much? Nine times out of ten, if he's asking you out, he's probably going to take you to somewhere nice on the resort."

I grabbed the outfit from her hands and went to the bathroom to shower and get prepared for this date. Knowing Kharisma, she wouldn't let this go until I went on this date with this man.

§

I sat across from this man and watched as he ordered for me. First, he made sure I didn't have any allergies, then he took over and ordered for me. The golf cart ride over to this side of the resort was filled with small talk and laughs. Kharisma made sure she stayed in my room until after I was on the golf cart. Colt brought me flowers to my bungalow and introduced himself to Kharisma, who was swooning at his New York accent. His accent was something to swoon about, however, she made it a big deal. I couldn't believe I was sitting here out to dinner with a man other than Phil. Since I had arrived here, I hadn't heard from Phil. He sent me emails to make sure we arrived safely, and after that, I hadn't heard too much from him.

"I appreciate you allowing me to order for you." He broke me from my thoughts. Flashing a smile, I picked up the Maui drink I had ordered.

"I've never had a man order my meal for me. You do this with all the ladies?" *What am I doing? I can't flirt with this man, I have a boyfriend*, I silently scolded myself. It was so hard not to flirt with this man.

"Only the ones I like," he smirked and tossed back the rest of his Hennessey. "I'm surprised you came out with me tonight."

"Well, my sister wasn't going to let me turn you down."

"I'm glad she's your sister," he chuckled.

The server brought over some sushi that Colt had ordered and some chopsticks. I watched as he handed me a chopstick and my own soy sauce, then bowed his head to pray. When he was done, he looked up at me and smiled before picking up his sushi with his chopstick effortlessly.

"Familiar with chopsticks?"

"Yeah, I spent two years in Japan when I was younger."

"Really, why?"

"I was young and trying to find myself, so I traveled for a while and then decided to settle in Japan. My moms was pissed, but it was the best time of my life."

"I've traveled, but I have never been bold enough to live anywhere except Atlanta."

"And why is that? Your boyfriend?" he mocked and I giggled as I took a bite from the sushi.

"My family and friends are in Atlanta, why would I ever leave?"

"Family and friends can visit. You gotta live your life, not because of your family."

I smiled. "Well, you don't know my family. We're very close-knit, and if I decided to move away, my mother would take it personal."

"It's always been me and my mom. My dad was here and there, but mostly, it was always me and my mother."

"Mama's boy," I joshed.

He chuckled and took another piece of sushi and chewed before he spoke. "How'd you meet your boyfriend?"

"Why do you keep mentioning my boyfriend?" I twirled my finger around one of my loose curls.

He smiled and chewed slowly again. "I'm just asking. He can't be too serious because you're on a date with me."

"This isn't a date. We're two adults enjoying dinner together." I set him straight. This was something strictly platonic. I wasn't interested in dating anyone except Phil.

"Why you get all dressed and shit? You should have come with what you had on at the bar?"

"Well, why did you go and get dressed in that linen suit?" I shot back. He looked great in his tan linen pants suit with a pair of leather Gucci sandals. He wore an understated gold chain that had a cross on it. He didn't seem like the flashy type, which I loved.

"Because I was taking a beautiful woman out on a dinner date. I could have come in some sweat shorts, sneakers and a tank top, but I was raised with more respect."

For the rest of dinner, we both ate and spoke about small things. He questioned me about my relationship and I volunteered what little information I wanted. He told me about his daughter and mother and listened. The conversation was great and it wasn't forced. By the end of dinner, I wasn't ready to end it. In the end, I was with another man and anything further than this dinner date would have been inappropriate, so I walked back to my bungalow — alone.

Chapter Four

TRYING TO MAKE IT WRIGHT

Colt

"Daddy, you need to wake up and take me to get my nails done," River nudged me as I laid in the bed, staring at the ceiling.

My mother had just sent me a text message on her way out to her friend's house, so I knew River was going to make it to my room to bother me next. It had been a week since I had been back from Bora Bora and I had only been doing quick flights that were no more than a two-hour trip. River had been busy with school and cheer that I hadn't spent much time with her. When my mother told me that she and her friend were going to the movies and lunch, I knew today was the day to spend some well-needed father and daughter time with River

"Damn, you don't know how to knock? What if I had a woman friend over?"

She held her hand on her hip and made a crook with her neck. "Daddy, you never have women friends. The last one wasn't around long because she wanted all your attention."

"Wait, how you know that?"

"I overheard Grammy telling Ms. Veronica over the phone," she informed and I shook my head.

My mother always felt the need to discuss my business with her little friends. I understood she wanted me to get married and live life again, but those things weren't on my mind. I was happy with my career, raising my daughter and being free to do whatever I wanted.

"Well, you need to stop listening to Grammy's conversations. What I tell you about grown folk business?" I sat up on the edge of my king size bed and stared at her.

Lowering her head, she replied, "Not to be in grown folk's business because that's what grown girls do."

"Exactly. You need your nails done, so go and take care of your morning hygiene so we can go and have brunch before the nail salon."

Quickly snapping her head up, she smiled at me and skipped toward the door. "Thanks, Dad."

I stood up, stretched and went to take care of my morning business before starting the day with River. At ten years old, my baby girl was starting to act like a damn teen already. She had to have her nails done every week and she had been on my ass about letting her dye her silky, natural curls. The shit had me bugging the fuck out because my little girl was becoming a young lady. I stared into the mirror and bent down to splash some water on my face. Since coming back from Bora Bora, I was struggling with focusing because I kept thinking about Happy. We spent one night together and that shit was magical. I hadn't had that kind of connection with a woman since River's mother passed away five years ago. When Tamia passed away, I never thought I could love another woman again. I mean, I wasn't in love with Happy or any shit like that, but the vibe I had with her that night had me thinking that if we continued to keep in touch, we could be something.

Tamia died a week after River had turned five years old. She had been battling ovarian cancer for two years and lost her battle. We all knew once she was diagnosed with stage four ovarian cancer that one day she was going to have to go. I prepared myself to lose my soulmate for two years while trying to work and care for her and our daughter. Tamia went through hell due to the chemo, losing her hair and always being sick after a treatment. Not to mention, the pain she dealt with on the regular was hard to watch. Towards the end, she was too weak to do anything and we had to move a hospital bed in our living room where she had an aide come twenty-four hours a day. I had to learn to administer morphine because the pain she felt was unbearable. The night before she died, I kissed her and spoke to her before I had to head out to work. I was flying from New York to Las Vegas and was scheduled to fly back home the following morning.

We laughed and she prayed like she usually did before I headed out to work. Tamia couldn't stand that I was a pilot and felt anxiety every time I had to go out and work. I liked being up in the air more than I liked being on the ground. Like usual, I kissed my mother and River on the way out and went to make money. With my mother not working, and Tamia unable to work, it was my money that paid the bills. If I would have known that by the time I landed in Las Vegas, I would get the call that she had passed on, I would have stayed home instead of going to work. Still, they paid me to fly planes, not catch feelings, so I had to suck up everything and do the job I was being paid to do. Tamia was more than my girlfriend, she was my child's mother and soulmate. Once in a lifetime, you meet someone who sweeps you off your feet, and who you can't live without. Tamia was the woman for me and cancer took her away from me and our daughter. Losing her was like losing a piece of my heart. Try explaining to a five-year-old that their mother is gone and never coming back.

Tamia would never be able to see our daughter go to prom, college, or walk the aisle and get married. She wouldn't be there to talk her off the ledge when a little raggedy-ass nigga was breaking her heart. I thought my heart hurt, but I had lived fine before meeting Tamia. River had never lived without her mother being in her life. My daughter was too young to understand and cried for her mother for an entire year. How do you move on without the person you planned to live the rest of your life with? You couldn't because every step you made in your life felt like you were deceiving that person.

When I decided to move us from our small apartment to a bigger one in Brooklyn, I felt like I was moving on and leaving Tamia behind. Living in that apartment that we brought River home in hurt like hell. Everything in that house reminded me of her and made me depressed. I couldn't turn a corner without thinking about her. Shit, I didn't want to forget about her, but thinking about her all the time felt like I was slowly dying.

"Daddy?" I heard River come into my bathroom.

Sticking my head out my master bathroom, I answered. "Yes, princess."

"Uhm, so should I wear these boots or these?" She held up two glitter boots that were the same, except they were different colors.

"Those." I pointed to the black glitter boots.

"Black? Ugh, you don't know better." She shook her head and retreated out of my bedroom.

Picking up my daughter and moving to Georgia was the scariest, yet exciting thing I had done in a long time. I went from just existing for River to trying to live again without Tamia. I was sure if I didn't have River, I would have done something extreme like move to another country and try to find myself. It was my daughter who kept me grounded. We all lived in a four-bedroom house in a subdivision that was one of the best in the city of Lawrenceville. My mother was able to have her own room and didn't have to share with River. My mother was a woman I could never repay for everything she had done for me. After Tamia died, I had to keep working and it was my mother who held down the fort and made sure I was able to work. She worried about me and often tried to get me to talk about my feelings, but that shit didn't do anything except make me angry. It wasn't Tamia's fault, yet I was angry at her. I guess you really did go through different steps of grieving and I was on anger. She had been gone for five years and I guess you could say I wasn't totally over her death yet. The trip to Bora Bora meant more to me than it meant to some. I went because it was the first trip I had taken after Tamia died.

"Daddy?" River popped back in my room and I looked at her with raised eyebrows, summoning her to speak. "How long are you going to take?" she questioned.

"I'm 'bout to shower and then we can head out. Why?"

"Oh, 'cause I'm hungry and I want to discuss my birthday party." She just had to remind me that she was turning eleven years old in a week.

"We can talk about it over brunch. I'll be done in a bit," I informed her and she turned on her heels to leave the room.

I kept staring across the table at River as she ordered for herself and handed the menu back over to the waitress. The waitress was so consumed with me, I prayed she got my baby's order right. If she was anything like her mama, she was going to have them send it back a million times until it was correct. She turned her attention to me with her pad and waited for me to order.

"I'll do the steak and eggs with wheat toast. Oh, and add a glass of orange juice, too." I ordered and handed her back the menu.

"We're pretty busy, but I'll make sure they get your food out quickly. Anything else I can get the two of you?" She paid no attention to River but gave all her attention to me.

"Nah."

"I hear an accent, where are you from?" she said in her thick southern drawl. "I've been trying to figure it out and can't," she giggled.

"New York," I replied, being short. Since moving down here, that was all I received. People wanted to know where I was from. Once I told them where I was from, they went on to ask me about New York and what brought me to Georgia. Usually when I told them I was a pilot, they were surprised. It was no secret that there weren't many black pilots out there.

"Oh my God, I've always wanted to visit New York... What do you sug—"

"Look, lady, I'm trying to spend time with my daughter. I'm sure if you Googled or did a poll on social media, you'd find the same shit I would waste twenty minutes telling you. I just want to connect with my baby girl while we're waiting for our food."

She looked embarrassed but played it cool. "I'm sorry. Your food should be out shortly, enjoy," she responded and scurried away.

"Daddy, that was rude." River called me out on my rudeness and I laughed.

"Baby girl, she was wasting my time."

"You tell me I should always be nice and you're the meanest of them all." She raised her eyebrow at me. I swear when she did that, she reminded me of her mother.

"Anyway, what did you want to talk about?"

She dug into her little purse and pulled out a small notebook. "My birthday. I have a list of friends and I want to do a skating party."

"Word? You hate skating."

"I know, but because I'm turning eleven, I'm doing a bucket list of things I want to do before I die."

Choking on my water, I looked at her like she had lost her mind. "You're turning eleven, not fifty, Riv."

"I saw it on a movie with Grammy and I want to do it. So, skating is something I hate and it's something I will do." She was adamant in what she was talking about, so who was I to stop her?

River had to grow up quicker than any child around. She had to understand situations that were far too complex for her to understand at such a young age. Because of that, she was forced to understand situations she should have never had to understand. River was wise for her age and understood way more than my mother and I gave her credit for.

"How many kids are you thinking about inviting to this party?"

"Dad, I know you just took off from work, but can you take off so you can be there for my party? I don't want to spend another birthday with just me and Grammy again." It hurt hearing her ask me something that should have been automatic.

The last birthday I spent with River was when she turned eight. I was always working, so I couldn't afford to take off from work and celebrate her birthday. It was either bills or being there to blow candles out for her. She tried to understand that I had to work and bring in the money, but I knew that even as young as she was, it didn't register as it should have. All she understood was that her father wasn't here and it was just she and her grandmother, celebrating another birthday alone. Money was better now and I didn't have to take any and everything that was available. I had taken the time off for River's birthday before she had even brought this up to me. When a child turned any number, it was a celebration. However, my baby girl was turning eleven and I was going to make sure I was there to spend it with her.

"You don't ask for much, so I guess I can make something happen."

A huge smile spread across her face, exposing her dimples. "Thank you, Daddy. I promise we're gonna turn up. Now, about my outfit. I'm thinking we should go shopping and find something so bomb." She started speaking fast, something she did when she was excited.

Like promised, our food came out pretty fast. Except, it wasn't the waitress who had taken our order. I chuckled to myself and reached across the table to hold River's hand so we could pray over our food.

"Amen." I lifted my head and we began to dig into our food. Like the little lady she was, she grabbed a knife and cut into her pancakes before she popped some into her mouth and chewed with her mouth closed.

"So, daddy... You never told me about your trip? How was it?"

"It was cool. I got to sleep in, eat, and do some fun things they had around the resort."

Chewing slowly, she placed her hand over her mouth before she spoke. "I missed you. Next vacation, can I go? Grammy told me you needed this, so I tried not to be mad."

"Most definitely. I was looking at some vacations we can do when you're out of school. What you think about Thailand?"

"Hmm, that can be fun."

"We'll continue to think on it and think of some fun places we can go. We can even bring Grammy, too," I suggested.

"Yes, because Grammy needs a break, too. We all can use one."

"Excuse you?"

"Dad, fifth grade is stressful. My science project gave me some gray hairs." She messed with her hair and I laughed.

"Little girl, you haven't hit stress yet."

"I have," she giggled. "When can me and Milani have a sleepover?" She spoke of Darrius' and his wife Kelli's daughter.

When we first moved here, we didn't know anyone, and because I worked with him, we decided to hang out outside of work. Darrius was cool as shit, and because he was originally from New York, we clicked like we had known each other our entire lives. His wife was sweet and tried to help as much as she could when it came to River. Whenever she and Milani did a mother and daughter date, she would make sure to include River, too, which I appreciated.

"I have to check with Darrius and Kelli. I'm sure you girls can get together at your birthday party."

"Can we make it a sleepover at a hotel?" She tried to toss that in.

"What the hell, you turn eleven once, right?" I gave in to her like I usually did.

My guilt took over and I tried to give River the world. If there was something I couldn't give her, I damn near tried giving it to her. It was something me and my mother constantly clashed over. She felt I spoiled River too much and needed to learn how to tell her no. I felt like because I was her only living parent, I *needed* to give her the world and didn't stop until I accomplished that. We continued to chat about her birthday and ate our food. With how much River was going on about her birthday, I knew I was about to be coming out of pocket for this little weekend of hers. It was my baby girl and I didn't mind doing that.

§

"Whew, what kind of day that child had?" My mother laughed as she came downstairs from getting River settled in bed for the night.

"We had brunch and was in the mall for six hours, only to leave with a pair of jeans she's still undecided on." I popped open a beer and rummaged through the fridge for leftovers.

"I can't believe she's growing up on us. She's so particular on what she wears. Reminds me of her mother."

"I told her that. Tamia would never toss on sweats, no matter how much I begged her to. Even when too weak to get out the bed, she made sure she was dressed every day." I smiled, thinking about my love.

My mother smiled and sat down at the kitchen table. "How are you doing, baby?"

"I'm good, mama, just trying to be here, there and everywhere."

"And who is here, there and everywhere for you, Colt? You haven't dated or taken anybody serious since Tamia died."

"Ma, let's not start this tonight." My mother felt because I didn't date and barely went out, besides work, that I was depressed or thinking about Tamia all the damn time. I thought about her from time to time, but how could I not? I was raising the smaller version of her.

"Colt, you know I worry about you. It's been about five years since Tamia left us and you haven't brought a woman around yet. I would ask if you're dating or sexual, bu—"

"Ma! Enough with this shit, man. I'm not worried about a woman who wanna fuck and then use me for my pockets. I care about my daughter and giving her the life I never had growing up!"

I slammed the fridge, snatched the beer up from the counter and retreated down to the basement where my man cave was.

I understood what my mother was worried about, and I could see her side of things, still, that didn't mean I was going to walk out and find a woman right away. Tamia was supposed to be my wife and now she was gone. It wasn't like she was some woman I met who had died the next day. We spent, planned and lived a life together. We had plans on buying a home, raising our daughter and having another sibling for River. Shit didn't work like that, and now here I was, trying to figure out how to proceed in life. Just because it had been a while since Tamia died, didn't mean I was supposed to be married with more kids, living happily ever after. Even if that did happen, the guilt would be too much for me to handle.

Flicking the TV on, I settled on some reality show that happened to already be on the TV and sipped my beer. I watched as the women fought about stupid shit and how their nails, clothes, and ass looked fake as fuck. The average woman men loved wasn't for me. I wasn't into women who had all those long-ass nails, fake asses, and all that weave. Give me a natural woman who was born with everything that was on her body. A weave here or there was cool with me but I didn't want a woman who felt she had to paint her face up just to grab some quick lunch. Natural beauty was what did it for me. I loved a woman who could put on some lip gloss, wet her hair and go about her business. When I thought about the type of woman I wanted, Happy Galleria came to mind.

Sitting across from her, sharing dinner, was the most fun I had on the trip to Bora Bora. I had gotten some me time away from everyone, but who wanted to visit an exotic island alone? She sat across from me with her natural, golden brown, curly hair carefree and her freckles on display. I guess all the sun caused them to pop more. She didn't wear a stitch of makeup and when she smiled, she lit up the dimly lit restaurant. Sitting up, I searched my desk for my iPad and pulled the case off to reveal the card she had handed me. Plopping back down on the couch, I grabbed my phone and dialed her number. The phone rang for a few, then her voice came through the line.

"Happy Galleria," she answered, sounding professional.

"I assume this is your professional line, huh?"

She laughed. I guess she recognized my voice. "Yes, it is. How can I help you, Mr. Wright?"

"Oh, I'm Mr. Wright?"

"Yes. Especially when you call my business phone." I could see the smile on her face just by hearing her voice.

"Boyfriend around?"

"We're in the middle of dinner. Can I give you a call tomorrow?"

"Oh, word? I just wanted to hit you up about my daughter's outfit for her birthday."

"Ohhh, okay. Gotcha."

"She can't decide and I happened to meet a fly-ass stylist, so I told her I would give her a call."

"I appreciate you reaching out. Can we meet for lunch to go over what look she's going for?"

"Ms. Galleria, do you always meet your clients on Sunday?"

"Only the clients I actually like. See you tomorrow. I'll shoot you a text with the place tomorrow."

"Looking forward," I smirked and ended the call.

I leaned back, guzzled the rest of my beer and looked at the TV. When I heard the top stair creek, I knew that meant my mother was coming down to finish speaking her peace. I didn't mind her meddling in my life because my mother wasn't that type. She usually felt the need to jump in when she felt she was needed. Like now, she felt the need to insert herself into my life because I wasn't dating or being bothered by women.

"I know you hear me, so don't you think of turning that TV up," she scolded and I laughed.

"Mama, I'm not even touching the remote." I placed the empty beer can down on the coffee table.

She came around the sectional and sat on the opposite side of the couch and stared at me before she spoke. "Colt, I worry about you. When I'm gone, who is going to care for both you and River?"

"You're not dying tomorrow. Ma, you being dramatic about this situation," I accused, and she touched her chest like she was appalled. "See, the dramatics, mama."

"All I'm saying is that I'm worried about you. It's been a while since you've dated and I know how important Tamia was to you. What about having more children or eventually getting married?"

"Eventually, I'll think about those things, mama. Right now, I'm not thinking about a woman, babies or marriage."

She sighed and leaned back in the couch. "I don't know what to do with you."

"Just love me, mama. That's all. I promise I'm working on myself and eventually, I'll be ready for all of that." If I had told my mother I met someone in Bora Bora, she would be on my ass about every small detail. Happy had a man and I wasn't trying to ruin that. When I was ready, I would get back into dating. Right now, I wasn't thinking about it. I knew one thing, for the first time in a while, I was looking forward to waking up early on my day off.

Chapter Five

WORKING OVERTIME

Happy

Since being back from Bora Bora, I had thrown myself right into work. I had a few clients who I was able to land while on vacation, so once I stepped foot back into Atlanta, I got to work. Phil had been busy with work and we had only seen each other occasionally. Last night, he asked me to come over and cook dinner with him. Even though I was still slightly pissed about my birthday dinner, I decided to put my best foot forward and show up to his apartment to try and mend what had been broken. Phil had kissed, hugged and showed me that he missed me, which warmed my heart. When I went to talk about my birthday dinner, he told me I needed to stop harping on the past and worry about our future. How could I worry about a future when I didn't know where we were going or what we were doing? Phil wanted things to go back to normal and that wasn't what I wanted to do. I was tired of always pushing my needs to the back because of his wants.

I stood in the bathroom, brushing my teeth while he got dressed for court. Last night should have been spent making love and being wrapped in each other's arms. Midway through cooking, Phil received a phone call and bailed to leave me to complete dinner. I thought we would have a candlelight dinner, but he was in his study, on the phone with his client. I ate dinner at his kitchen island, soaked in his tub, then went to bed. While tossing and turning, I thought about the call I'd received from Colt. I was shocked to hear from him. After our small dinner, I didn't think I would ever hear from him again. Hearing his deep baritone voice come through my phone line sent chills through my body. I was glad that Phil was busy in his study when he called because he would have questioned who was calling me on my work phone this late.

"Baby, did you hear what I said?"

I removed my toothbrush from my mouth and looked up at him through the mirror. "Huh?"

"You mean, excuse me, babe. Since when do you respond by saying *huh*?" I spit out the toothpaste and rinsed my mouth before I turned to face him.

"Yes, babe. What did you say?"

"I was reminding you about the gala that my firm is throwing tomorrow night. Did you get your dress and line up your makeup artist and hairstylist?"

I had done all of those things when he mentioned it last month. This gala was all he kept talking about. Phil didn't give a damn about the kids with cancer they were raising money for. He was more concerned with showing up and looking so amazing, it left a lasting impression on his boss. Phil worried more about what his boss thought than me.

"Yes. I have to go pick up my dress later on today."

"And what about my suit?"

"That, too."

"Good. I'm glad your little hobby is messing around in clothes. You always keep me so sharp." He bent down and kissed me on the lips before he headed out of the bathroom.

"Hobby? Phil, this is my career." I followed him out the bathroom. He stared at me as he pulled his suit jacket on.

"Babe, your career was when you worked at Galleria's. You made such good money working with your family and you left that for what?"

"Because I wasn't happy and my father didn't give me the creative control I need. You love your job, Phil."

"No, I love the money and lifestyle my job affords me. It's been six months, babe. You need to go speak to your father about letting you have your job back."

"What does that even mean? It's been six months, what?" What did he mean it had been six months? It had been six months and I had been busting my ass to make sure I did what needed to be done to keep my head afloat. Of course I had a trust fund and savings, so it wasn't like I was hurting for money.

"Happy, it's been six months and you've spent more time in your home than anywhere else. You have clients, but not that many, and I can tell you're not happy."

Slamming my hand on the dresser, I looked Phil straight in the eyes. He had to be joking with the shit he was saying out of his mouth. "I'm not begging for money. Phil, you tend to forget that I have a huge social media following and blog. My client list is growing every day. I actually have one I'm meeting today for lunch."

When I stared into his eyes, I could tell he didn't give a damn about my career. To him, I was playing around in clothes and wasn't pursuing a career. It hurt that the man I loved and wanted to spend the rest of my life with didn't have any respect for my career choice. When it came to him, I respected and showed up for him in every aspect of his career. I was his biggest cheerleader and often sacrificed things in our relationship for the sake of his career. All I wanted was the same respect when it came to my career, and I never received it. Even when I worked with my dad, he would make snide comments about me working for family, so it wasn't the same amount of pressure he had when trying to prove himself at his job.

"I'm not going to argue with you, Happy. All I'm saying is that you need to think about the future. You want to be married and have children, well, all those things cost money. You living off your savings and trust fund isn't ideal for me. I'm a grown man, and while I don't mind taking care of our home, in the future, I refuse to have you sitting around while I'm working. I'm running late and you know the traffic, we'll talk tonight over dinner." He kissed me on the forehead, grabbed his wallet, and headed out of the bedroom.

That was another thing that pissed me off about Phil. He always felt that when he was done with a conversation, that was when it ended. He didn't care about what anyone else had to say. He was done and didn't want to hear any more. He made it seem like I lounged around in my pajamas and paid my bills from my trust fund account. I made money from clients. It wasn't enough to pay all my bills, but it was something that added to my account every month. I followed him to the front of his condo and he was already grabbing his briefcase and holding onto the doorknob.

"Babe, we'll talk later. Enough," he dismissed like he often did. With those parting words, he closed the door behind him, leaving me to stand in my robe, feeling defeated. I shook back the tears and went to get myself ready for the day.

I sat with my legs crossed, shaking my foot, annoyed because Colt was running ten minutes late. I had arrived at the Egg Harbor Café twenty minutes early so I could prepare myself to meet with this fine-ass man. A man as fine as Colt, you needed some minutes to get yourself together and make sure you didn't stutter or get lost in his dreamy, light brown eyes. When I sat across from him in Bora Bora, I had to keep myself from getting lost in everything he said. I ordered a fruit parfait and waited another five minutes before I pulled my phone out to remind him of the meeting he had called me to arrange. Just as I was entering my passcode, he strolled into the café wearing a brown leather jacket, cream sweater, distressed jeans and a pair of Timberland boots. If I didn't know better, I would have assumed this man was a stylist himself with the outfits he pulled together.

"I'm always on time and I apologize for being late," he apologized and reached down to give me a quick hug.

"My time is valuable, Colt," I reminded him. He apologized and I could have left it alone, but he needed to know that my time was worth something.

"I know, and that's why I apologized. My alarm didn't go off and traffic was a bitch getting here."

"Don't you live here close?"

"Nah, I live in Lawrenceville."

"Really? I had looked at a few homes there when I was buying my home." I sat up and crossed my legs in the opposite direction.

"Word? Why didn't you decide to buy there?"

"I like to be in the city and my sister doesn't live too far from me." I finished speaking just as the waiter came over to take our order.

"Welcome to Egg Harbor Café, what can I get you both to drink?" He smiled and looked at both of us in the eyes. The staff here was always impeccable. I loved when a place had amazing staff because it made me want to come back. I didn't care how good the food was, if the staff sucked, then I would never dine at the establishment again. Colt looked at me to order.

"I've already ordered. Remember... you were late."

"Ah, you got jokes. I'll take a coffee. Black with two teaspoons of sugar and a drop of honey," Colt ordered.

"I'll get that right out to you." He jotted it down in his notebook quickly, then turned to complete Colt's order.

My personal phone buzzed and I quickly answered it. "Hey."

"Babe, did you get me a red tie? It has to be red because that's the theme of the gala," Phil questioned without greeting me.

"You told me you didn't care. I can see about the tie when I pick it up later," I huffed into the phone. After this morning, I knew a few days away from him was needed.

"I didn't tell you anything," he tried to argue, and I waved the white flag quickly.

"I'll call you when I arrive at the shop. Bye, Phil," I said through gritted teeth. Phil wanted everything to go off without a hitch because he had convinced my father to become a sponsor and donate some money to the children.

"Trouble in paradise?" Colt raised an eyebrow and I stared right into his eyes. His eyes were kind and made me feel safe – even if it was temporary.

"I'm just tired. I'm twenty-nine years old, running around, being a girlfriend to a man who is more concerned about his career."

"Can't rush things like that, sweetheart. The last thing you want is to end up in a marriage you wish you never got involved in. Let that man do it when he's ready because ain't shit worse than a man forced into marriage." The waiter set his coffee down and he thanked him, then sent him on his way.

"It's been four years and I just want more. I'm tired of being his girlfriend. I want a life with him. Children, a home, and all those things that come with marriage." Here I was, sitting in a café, having a conversation with a client about how unhappy I was about my current life.

"Four years isn't all that long. Shit, you don't know a person until you're four years into the relationship. He makes you happy?"

"Sometimes."

"Life too short to only be happy some of the time."

I ran my hand through my curls and sighed. "I'm unhappy. It's ironic that my name is the emotion I want to feel the most, but I'm the opposite. I'm tired of always sacrificing things that I want. My career isn't where I thought it would be, I'm unhappy in my relationship, and I spend my nights cuddled in bed, binge-watching old sitcoms. And, why I'm telling you this makes no sense. I'm sorry," I quickly apologized.

It felt nice having someone else to talk to about my issues. Kharisma listened, but she didn't just listen. She always had to have a solution that she wanted me to follow. Then, Jade, she was so absent, she didn't know what was going on with my life. She was living her own life with the man she thought was the man of her dreams. Having someone who didn't know me, my relationship, and didn't judge felt nice during a venting session.

"Nah, you good. I'm a good listener."

"You probably don't have these issues because women want to toss their panties right at your feet."

He shrugged. "So, you think I'm cute?"

I blushed and looked away because the smirk on his face had me feeling a way I shouldn't be feeling. "I didn't say that. All I said was that you probably had women all over you."

"Nah, I'm not worried about women right now."

"So, men?"

"Fuck you!" He laughed and took a sip from his coffee. "Nah, I haven't found the right woman yet."

"What do you look for in a woman?"

"You know somebody?"

"Hell, I might. I have a lot of friends and these women are businesswomen, not someone looking to fish around in your pockets."

"What about my pants?"

"You are gross. I'm serious."

"Shouldn't we be talking about your stylist services?"

I smiled and put my iPad back into my purse. It was clear he didn't come here for me to work for him. "Let's be real. You didn't call me last night because you needed me to pull some clothes for your daughter."

"Hell yeah, I did. You ever spent six hours with a ten-year-old in a mall, and leave with a pair of jeans?"

"Yep, I have a client who hates everything until I pick the same exact items up the next day when she's not with me."

"Shit, how the fuck you do it? Thought I was about to die and shit."

"Patience and my love for fashion. So, you did call for my

services, huh?" I smiled and licked the coconut yogurt off my spoon.

He finished his coffee and flashed his beautiful white smile. "I'm fucking with you. I called you to see you again."

"The fact that I had a boyfriend didn't cross your mind once when you called me?"

"Nah."

"Why not? I'm really in a serious relationship."

"Are you? You knew why I called this meeting, and you still came." He looked under the table and licked his lips. "Put them red peep toes on just to turn me on, eh?"

This should have been inappropriate, and I should have put him in his place out of respect for my boyfriend, yet I didn't. I blushed, flirted, and messed with the loose strand of my hair as he licked his lips and fed me compliments.

"I dress bomb every day of the week. It's kind of my walking résumé. Anyway, what kind of woman are you looking for?" I repeated my question to him again.

Deep down, I wanted to see if I was the type of woman he was looking for. I didn't know why I cared when I was in a relationship with Phil. "Smart, beautiful, about her business and wanting to settle down. I don't like a woman who wants to play games and wants me to play fucking charades to figure her out. Be open with me, and I'll do the same," he explained. "You gotta friend for me?"

"I may."

"Can I be honest?"

"Sure."

"I don't give a fuck about your boyfriend," he bluntly stated and stared at me.

"Huh?"

"I don't care that you have a boyfriend. Since the day you sat your pretty ass across from me in Bora Bora, I've been wanting to kick it to your further." He leaned forward and spoke while staring right into my eyes.

"I have a bo—"

"I hear what your mouth is saying, but your body is telling me something else."

I mixed the berries into my yogurt and took a spoonful into my mouth. What he was saying was true. My mouth was telling him I had a boyfriend, but between my legs spoke another tune. I was imagining us in so many different positions, my head was about to spin.

"Colt, we need to be professional. What happened in Bora Bora was a simple dinner date. You know I was involved in a situation before I even agreed to have dinner with you."

"Tell me that he makes you feel good, and I'll stop."

I couldn't bring my mouth to say how good Phil made me feel, because the truth of the matter was, he didn't. He was sweet when he wasn't busy, and sex was mediocre. He was always rushing to get himself off, and I usually pleased myself in the shower with his showerhead. It was sad to say that his showerhead had a better tongue game than he did.

"I can't dis—"

"Ma, I came here for two things. I need you to help me with my daughter's outfit for her party this weekend, and I came to see you again. Since we parted ways, you've been on my mind."

"Well, can I meet with your daughter so I can get an idea of things she likes?"

"Sparkle, glitter, and did I mention sparkle?" he laughed.

I grabbed my pen and agenda out of my purse and jotted down what he told me about his daughter. "I can pull some options and bring them by this week. Shoot me over her sizes and I can get to work."

"Bet." The way he had this hood aura about him but was able to turn it off and be professional was sexy as hell. The day he spoke to everyone on the plane, I wouldn't have ever guessed he had this side of him.

"Is that a yes?"

"Yeah. You gonna come to my crib and bring the clothes?"

"Uh-huh," I replied as I continued to jot down the notes he

told me about his daughter. I knew the perfect place to find her some pieces.

"Are you trying to go for the designer look or...?"

"Nah, she's eleven. I'm not trying to break my pockets on some designer clothes that she's just going to outgrow next year."

"I understand. I'll pull some good pieces that won't have you going in the red."

"Appreciate it. Business is out the way, so can we have another dinner date?"

I laughed and packed my agenda back into my purse. "Colt, you already know the situation. Shoot me your address and I'll come over to bring the things for your baby girl. I'm good at my job, so I'm sure she'll love everything I pick out, so get your credit card prepared." I stood up and walked near him.

He rubbed the side of my thigh and looked up at me. "We'll definitely be seeing each other again." He stood up and bent down to kiss me on the cheek.

My legs were like rubber as I tried to walk out of the café. I walked down the street to my car and took a deep breath when I got behind my wheel. Colt Wright made me feel like everything was right – no pun intended.

§

I sat in the mirror and put on the thirty thousand dollar diamond earrings that a local jewelry boutique here in Atlanta had lent me for the gala. I wore an emerald satin gown that touched the floor and dragged behind me. I paired it with a pair of shoes that matched the color of the gown exactly. My hair was straightened and pulled up into an updo that showed off my features. On my neck sat a diamond chain that Phil had given me for our first year anniversary. He told me it cost more than some people's salary. Money didn't impress me because I had grown up with a bunch of it. My sisters and I had gone to some of the best schools Atlanta had to offer, our first cars were Range Rovers when we each turned fifteen, and our father had handed us each a credit card that we could use whenever we wanted. Money didn't mean much to me, and a man who had some didn't make me bat an eyelash.

The reason I fell in love with Phil wasn't because he came from money, his career, or what he could do for me. It was his drive and how committed he was to accomplishing his dreams. Phil's father was a retired defense attorney and owned a law firm that was also very well known. Phil could have easily decided to work for his father where his name was already on the door. Instead, he went to the competition, worked himself up, and wanted to gain the title of partner on his own. That was what made me fall in love with him. Who would have known the same reason I fell in love with him was the same reason our relationship was in jeopardy?

"You look stunning, Happy Galleria." Phil walked into his bedroom and stared at me through shocked eyes.

I turned around and smiled.

"I am. I can feel that partner position. I've already donated more than fifty thousand dollars to the charity."

"Fifty thousand dollars? Phil, that's a bit much."

"I need to show Klein I'm serious about all the work I've been doing. If it all goes well, I'll be making that back with my new salary as partner."

"That's not the point. You should donate because you want to help these children, not to become partner at the firm."

"Happy, tonight is not the night for arguing. I'm already stressed and I haven't stepped into the room. Your parents still coming, correct?"

"Yes."

My parents were coming because they were really into giving back and donating to charities. We had our own charity for under-privileged families. My father didn't always have money and always reminisced on the hardships his parents went through to put food on the table for him and his siblings. It was something that was near and dear to his heart. I believed that was why my father was so blessed. He had a huge heart and would give the shirt off his back to someone in need. It was one of the things I loved about my father. The kind and giving man he was was the reason he was blessed in all aspects of his life. So, even if I hadn't invited him, he would have been invited because everyone knew he loved to donate to charity.

"Perfect. We should get going. We're sharing a limo with my parents," he informed me last minute.

Phil's parents were sweet and I loved them to death. His mother always brought up the subject of marriage whenever Phil and I were around, but he ignored her, just like he ignored me. The ride to the gala would be interesting because his parents, just like mine, wanted grandchildren. I was tired of them always bombarding me with questions about when I was going to become a wife or have children like it was only up to me. Phil didn't get bombarded with these questions because he usually had to take a call or just wasn't present in the conversation at all.

"I haven't seen your parents since my birthday dinner."

"I'm sure they'll be glad to see you." He touched the small of my back as we headed out of his condo. Like usual, Phil had this phone attached to his ear as soon as we exited the elevator. Apparently, one of his colleagues was having an emergency that needed his expertise. The Lincoln Navigator limo was waiting right in front of the condominium with his parents inside. The driver held the door open for me and I scooted in and Phil scooted in behind me.

"Happy, how are you, sweetie?" His mother scooted closer to me to hug and kiss me on the cheek. "As always, you look fabulous," she complimented.

As much as I wanted to return the compliment, I couldn't. Kendra loved to brag on her stylist anytime we spoke about my career as a stylist. She loved the work and pieces she constantly pulled for her, so who was I to judge what she was wearing? Except, her outfit looked a hot mess and she needed to fire her stylist and hire me.

"I'm doing great. You know me, staying busy and working."

"How was Bora Bora?"

"Beautiful. I had such an amazing time with my sister. It was a well-needed trip away from everything."

"Next time you need to bring Phil along. Maybe it'll be during your honeymoon." She giggled and tapped her son's knee.

Phil looked up from his phone and smiled, then put his head back down into his phone. When I looked across the limo, his father was doing the same exact thing; his face fully focused on his phone that was right in his hands.

"We shall see. Whenever Phil is ready, he'll do it."

"He needs to hurry up. I want grandchildren, and neither of you are getting any younger."

This was what I hated about being around his parents. I should say his mother because his father never paid much attention. Usually, he just agreed with whatever she said. Phil and his father were cordial, still, you could tell there was tension between them. Phil betrayed the family when he decided to go and work for the enemy. His father had paid for years of college for him to take over the family's law firm, and Phil did the opposite. I understood why Phil did what he did and admired him for wanting to build his legal career on his own. His father didn't understand and it was often the topic of conversation whenever we did get together with his family.

The ride to the gala didn't take long. I spent time talking to his mother about the redecorating she was doing in her home. Hearing about her new guest bedroom was more entertaining than hearing her ask me questions about what Phil and I were doing and when we were going to settle down. I was sick of having to explain my life and our plans to everyone when Phil got off without having to deliver an explanation to anyone. I reached my hand out of the limo and Phil kissed me on the cheek just as the photographer snapped a picture.

"Baby, you look ravishing," he complimented while whispering in my ear. I smiled as the photographer took another picture and we headed inside the venue.

As soon as we made our way into the venue, I spotted my sister across the room. Kharisma was here because it had to do with children and she loved children. My sister Jade wasn't back in the country, which didn't surprise me at all. She was the one sister who was never home and always around her fiancée. With her career, it made me wonder how she took that much time off and her business didn't take a hit. Jade was a wedding planner and she was a good one. If and when Phil decided to pop the question, it was my big sister who would plan my wedding. Except, she was so into her fiancé's life, she barely made time for her own company. She had a staff who ran things for her, however, she was never doing work. The waiting list to have Jade Galleria plan their wedding was as long as this dress I was currently wearing. Each of my sisters was self-made and didn't need a man. Still, in the name of me, we were all stupid.

"Hi, Phil, can I talk to my sister really quick?"

"Kharisma, you look stunning. How's the practice?" He tried to make small talk, and Kharisma wasn't the least interested in playing catch up with him.

"Thank you." She smiled and gently pulled me by my arm, over to the ice bar. "So, Mom and Dad aren't going to be able to make it," she informed me.

"Something wrong?"

"Dad has a colleague coming into town and agreed to have dinner with him. He did send over a check for the charity."

"And Mom?"

"Well, you know Mom doesn't go anywhere without Dad. More than likely, she's going to be with Dad."

"I need to talk to you." I switched gears. With all the running around I had done today, I didn't have time to speak with my sister about the meeting I had with Colt.

"You okay?" A concerned expression came across her face.

"I'm fine. I had lunch with Colt."

Kharisma's face lit up like a Christmas tree. "Oh em gee, you're so bad." She hit me gently on the arm. "How did it go?"

"It's not like that." I accepted a drink from the bartender who was pressed to hand me the event's signature drink.

"Well, what is it like? You went out with him again. Something has to be going on." She took a drink from the bartender.

"He wants me to style his daughter."

"Nope, he wants you. He wasn't thinking about hiring a stylist for his daughter before he met you."

"Khar, I feel like I almost cheated on Phil today. Like... the words he was saying and how he caressed my thigh then kissed me on the cheek. Kharisma, I was flirting back with him." I put my hand to my face and sighed.

"Yess, Happy! How did it feel?"

"I'm pretty sure my panties were soaking wet. That man made my legs shake as I bolted out of there and headed to my car."

Kharisma was so wrapped into what I was saying, she hadn't noticed Phil walk up behind her. "You need to see him aga—"

"See who?" Phil asked as he placed his arm around my waist. My subtle signal went over her head.

"A friend," she dryly replied.

"Who is this friend?" Phil let everything go over his head, but the one time he caught the tail end of a conversation, now he wanted to know everything that was going on and who we were talking about?

"Babe, how are things going? Have you seen Klein yet?" I tried to switch the subject and I could tell from his face we would be revisiting the subject at a later date.

"Yes, that's why I came over to grab you. He wants to meet you." He guided me away from my sister.

"Why do they want to meet me?" I asked him as we made our way across the ballroom and over to the short, black man with a bald head. He was standing beside a tall, light-skinned model type of woman.

If this woman was his wife, I was almost certain she was using him for the money. "Klein, this is my girlfriend. Happy, this is my mentor and boss." He introduced me to the infamous Klein. He wanted me to shake the hand of the man who always needed Phil at his beck and call. The reason we could never have a decent night out on a date. I knew Phil was to blame, too, but it was Klein who made him pick up the phone and hold hour-long conversations in the middle of our date nights.

"Nice to meet you, Mr. Klein." I smiled and shook his hand.

"What you say her name is again?" he asked in his thick southern accent.

"Happy Galleria," I repeated, like he hadn't heard the first time.

"Oh, a Galleria... Is your father here?"

"No, he has other obligations tonight, but he sends his donation and love," I replied.

Phil took over with his ass kissing and went on and on about how he loves being a part of the company. I sat there and kept motioning for the bartender to bring me drink after drink. My mind was on Colt, and part of me couldn't wait to see him tomorrow when I brought the clothes I had picked out for his daughter's birthday party.

Chapter Six

YOU WANNA BE RIGHT OR BE WITH ME?

Colt

"Yo, you wilding if you think I'm 'bout to fly with Captain Underpants," Darrius complained about our co-worker. He couldn't stand the man because his ass crack was always hanging out of his pants. Anytime we flew with him, Darrius ignored anything the man said.

Like today, he should have been over some damn ocean, flying to Dubai, and he was sitting in his garage, drinking a beer and venting to me about the man. I guzzled the rest of my beer and stared at him with a blank expression. This nigga Darrius had a wife, daughter, and a newborn son, and his ass was worried about another man who wasn't worried about his ass. I had to remind myself that he was younger than me and that it would eventually kick in for him.

"D, you need to stop worrying about Captain Underpants and get your bread, man. You worried about him and he's clocking his hours," I reminded him.

"Hell, I couldn't fly anyway. Kelli is due any day now and I want to be here for my son," he replied.

"Kelli is eight months, the hell you talking about? And last I saw her, she was still going to the gym and being active. You trying to use your wife as an excuse? Nah, that's low... even for you."

"Yeah, what-the-fuck-ever. You know I hate doing long flights, especially if you're not working. Anyway, what's going on with the girls? Your mama called Kelli to tell her about some sleepover." He reminded me of River's birthday weekend in a few days.

I reached into his fridge and grabbed another beer. Before cracking it open, I spoke. "Yeah, she's having a little roller-skating party with their school friends, and then she wants to have a sleepover with Milani," I explained further.

"Milani hasn't stopped talking about this weekend. Her mother went out and swiped that damn American Express card on a new outfit. And what makes it worse is that I can't complain because she'll toss the baby into the shit, too, and make me look like I'm the bad guy," he complained further.

Darrius was twenty-seven and he was a junior flight pilot. He never actually flew the plane, besides if someone took a break. He always nagged me to allow him to take off and land and I always turned him down. He was more like the little brother who always got into shit, and you had to pull him out of trouble. I didn't know how many times I had to stop him from arguing with pilots who were higher rankings than him. He acted like he didn't have a family to provide for.

"Happy wife, happy life," was all I replied. When Darius got to talking about how much money his wife spent, he spent our entire get together chatting about Kelli. I knew more about how much Kelli spent in Victoria's Secret than I cared to.

"Yeah, the sucka who said that shit didn't have bills."

"How's the house shopping going?" I switched gears because I didn't want a recap of how much Kelli had spent for the month.

"It's going." He shrugged like he didn't care.

"Going?"

"Yeah. She wants some big house and I'm cool with getting a townhouse or a condo. Not like we need all that space."

"Man, you living in Atlanta, Georgia, do you really want to live in some cramped-ass apartment? Y'all about to have a baby and he need space, plus Milani is getting older and you know how girls are."

"Buying a house together seems so... final," he admitted.

"Final?"

"Like, I already got the ball and chain, and now I'm 'bout to be locked into a mortgage for thirty years. That shit is enough for me to run like hell."

"You and Kelli been together since you were younger. If you gotta get locked down with anybody else, wouldn't you want it to be with her?"

He drank some of his beer, then looked at the mounted TV in the garage. "I want to stay in this rental and she talking about she need more space. What more space she need, man?"

Darrius and Kelli rented a starter home with two bedrooms and a one-car garage. While I tried to see things Darrius' way, I knew they needed the space. He just wasn't ready to get locked into a mortgage with his wife of almost a year. Although they had been together since they were younger, Kelli told him to either give her a ring, or she was leaving him. Darrius rushed to put a ring on her finger and promised her the wedding of her dreams after she had the baby.

"Have you spoke to her about how you feel?"

His eyes widened and he stared at me for a second before he replied. "Man, have you ever spoke your feelings to a pregnant woman?"

"Yeah, and she handled them well."

"Well, that ain't damn Kelli. She cries, gets dramatic, and tries to leave the damn house." He grabbed a handful of chips from the bowl on the coffee table. "Plus, she wanna move and go shopping like we not planning this huge-ass wedding." He continued to complain about the shit I prayed for.

Darrius had a beautiful wife and daughter, a house that his wife made a home, and a son on the way. Each time we spoke, he always complained about shit we had to do as adults.

"You promised her this wedding."

"Yeah, that's before I knew I would be dropping over twenty grand. I'm a junior pilot, not fucking El Chapo."

Hey, I'm heading to the address you sent me. I think I picked out some amazing pieces and can't wait to meet your princess and show her these pieces.

Happy's text popped across my screen while Darrius continued to vent.

As soon as I read her text message, I chugged the rest of my beer and tossed the bottle into the recycling bin. "Man, you complain too much. Remember that chick from the plane before I left for vac—"

"You cracked that?" he cut me off with excitement.

"Nah, it's not even like that. We ended up staying at the same resort and had dinner one night."

"And... you cracked after dinner?"

"Fool. Get your mind out the gutta. I didn't sleep with that woman, I don't even get down like that."

"Shit, if I was single, I'd be hitting something in every city I touch down in." He daydreamed about the life he thought I wanted to live.

"Man, I'm looking for a wife. I'm not looking for some woman I'll fuck and never see again."

"Yeah, yeah... what happened with her?"

"I ended up calling her to help me find River a birthday outfit. She's a stylist... her family actually owns Galleria stores."

"Niggaaaa! She loaded." He jumped out his chair and stared at me. "You landed a damn millionaire. The Galleria family is fucking well known here and they got bankroll."

"I don't give a damn about her having millions."

"How the hell did her pampered ass end up finding *your* daughter clothes for her birthday? Shouldn't yo' ass be picking out her clothes or flying her daddy's private jet? He just donated a million dollars to some charity gala that was going on here."

"Why the fuck do you know so much about the Galleria family?"

"All Atlanta news do is talk about that damn family. Look, date her and then ask her for thirty thousand... you know, nothing too big. Give me twenty and boom! Kelli can get her dream wedding."

I laughed because he was serious. "It ain't even like that. She got a man."

"And?"

"She's pretty serious about him. Wants a ring and everything from him."

"Bruh, why everybody wanna get married? That's beside the point. I could tell from your smirk you don't give a damn about her man."

"Possibly."

"She agreed to have dinner with you so she must have been feeling you or some shit."

I shrugged and stood up. "I don't know. I'm not rushing her, but letting her see that if she want a real man, I'm right here."

"Her family owns a damn private jet, you think she want a nigga who flies planes for Delta?"

"She wasn't on a private jet when I bumped into her ass, now was she?"

"The jet probably wasn't fueled. Either way, she's used to money and don't want to live like us."

"Like us? Man, I drive a new Jeep Grand Cherokee, I live in a nice house in a nice subdivision and my daughter goes to private school. My bills are paid, my mama taken care of, and I got money in my account. I live well and I'm blessed, so I'm never gonna complain about how I live."

I was born and raised in the hood. For years, I struggled to give my family the life I was able to give them now. Working hard and having tunnel vision was what had gotten me here. If I wasn't enough for shorty, then she wasn't the woman for me and I needed to look elsewhere.

"That's not what I'm saying. She's probably used to maids and all that stuff. Being with a dude who don't drive a foreign probably gonna shock the shit out of her."

Ten minutes away.

Happy sent another text message and I grabbed my keys off the coffee table.

"D, I'll holla at you next week. We got a flight to London," I reminded him and headed inside his house. Because his garage doubled as his man cave, he never opened the garage doors.

"See ya!" he yelled behind me.

When I walked through the kitchen, I found Kelli with her wedding planning books, humming along to her wedding playlist. I knew this because this was what she did every time I came over. She was adamant about having the wedding five months after the baby was born.

"Hey, Colt, how are you?" She smiled and stood up to hug me.

"Can I?" I asked before touching her stomach.

"Boy, you ask every time you go and touch my stomach. Of course, it's fine." She stood there and allowed me to touch her stomach. Pregnancy was so beautiful on women. It gave them this glow they could never achieve with makeup.

"He's getting so big. You excited for him to come?"

"Not really. I wanted to be in a new place. I have a bassinet, but no bedroom for him. We're outgrowing this place and it's a constant argument with Darrius." She cut her eyes and sat back down.

"We just gotta pray for him, Kelli. You know your husband is stubborn."

"Yes, so stubborn," she sighed. "Anyway, we're ready for River's party and sleepover." She switched the conversation.

"River won't stop talking about Milani coming over. You know I appreciate you for staying with the girls at the hotel."

"I don't mind. My sister is bringing my nieces over, so it'll be a real party messing with the girls."

"River better not ask for anything until her next birthday. I already have to go meet this stylist who is putting together her birthday look."

"Ahkae, River. Go ahead, girl," she laughed. "Let me not hold you, see you soon." I bent down and kissed her on the cheek.

Happy had sent me a message and told me she had arrived in front of my house, so I rushed from Darrius' house to make it home. We lived fifteen minutes from each other, so I turned into my subdivision in record time. When I pulled up to my house, there was a black Tesla parked in my driveway. My moms always parked in the garage, so I pulled up beside her car and hopped out. She was sitting in her car, and when she realized I had pulled into the driveway, she opened the door and stepped out. When she stepped out, it was like time stood still for a brief moment.

She wore a black plaid dress, black velvet thigh-high boots and carried a Givenchy purse in her hand, while a pair of black sunglasses sat on her face. Her natural golden curls were all over her head and she wore red lipstick. It was hard for me to focus when she stepped out her car looking so fucking good. I knew she was here to help us find something for River, but I wasn't interested in finding my daughter's clothes, I was more interested in Happy Galleria standing in front of me.

"Are you just going to stand there and drool, or are you going to greet me?" She smiled as she placed her purse on top of her car, then opened the back door of her car.

"I mean, you show up like this and expect me not to react?"

"This?" She looked down. "I just tossed this on because I was supposed to have brunch with my sister. Long story short, she bailed." She pulled out garment bags out of the car.

"If that's how you go to brunch, then I don't wanna see what you gonna wear out to dinner."

"Oh, shush," she blushed and bent over and grabbed two shoe boxes. "Are you going to help or stare at my ass?"

“I wasn’t looking at your ass. My mother didn’t raise me like that.”

“Hmm, I bet.” She giggled and handed me over the garment bags. “Show me the way.”

“River and my mom should be coming any minute. She got out of school twenty minutes ago and they usually stop for Starbucks before they head home.”

“I like her already. Starbucks is my favorite place to grab some coffee from,” she replied as she followed me into the house.

She stood in the foyer and looked around. I could tell she was making mental notes as I took her into the living room. “Want something to drink?”

“Um, I’ll take some water.”

“Ight,” I replied and headed into the kitchen. Because the kitchen was an open concept, I was able to watch her while I grabbed her a glass of water. She stood with her arms folded, looking at the pictures on the fireplace.

“It’s been you and your mother your entire life, huh?”

“Yeah. Pretty much. Then River came.”

“You all live under the same roof?” she inquired and accepted the water. I watched as she took a sip and stared up at me.

“Yeah. It’s just me and River, and I’m always gone for work, so it made sense.”

“I’m not judging, I just couldn’t imagine living with my parents. I love them dearly, but my mother has ways that make me want to live far away.”

I smirked. “What did you bring for my baby girl?”

“Nope, I’m not opening anything until the client arrives.”

“Client? The hell you mean? I’m paying.”

“And she’s picking.” She giggled and placed the glass down onto the coaster on the coffee table. “Where’s her room? I want to get everything ready so when she walks through the door, she’s mesmerized. Just because Dad is picking up the tab, doesn’t mean I’m not going to treat her like every other client.”

I chuckled and pointed upstairs. “Come on.” She followed me

upstairs to River's bedroom. My daughter was a girly girl. Everything was either pink or purple in her room. She loved everything about being a girl and my credit cards reflected that with her little shopping trips.

"Wow, her room is really pink." She placed the garment bags on the bed. "My room was the same way when I was younger. My father had this painter come and paint a huge pink bow with glitter behind my canopy bed." She reminisced about her childhood.

I sat down in River's pink computer chair. "Oh, yeah? What made you go into the fashion field?"

"I love any and everything about clothes. You can be whoever you want with clothes. I can dress a homeless woman up in thousand dollar clothes and people will think she's rich."

"So you want to front, basically?"

"No, I like the illusion of being someone I'm not. When people see me, they don't see the woman who is unhappy, on the verge of a breakdown every other day and simply trying to hold it all together. They see this woman who just walked through their doors wearing this season's Fendi boots paired with a bomb outfit. Clothes are like my..." She snapped her fingers. "Cape."

When she explained why she loved clothes so much, it made sense to me. "Why you so unhappy?"

"That's another topic for another day. Today is about your daughter, plus, you already know some of it."

"Some of it? Tell me more over dinner."

She blushed and tried to busy herself with the clothes. "Colt, you know my situation." She turned and hung the dress on the closet door.

In one swift movement, I was behind her. When she turned around, she jumped. "I also know your situation doesn't make you happy."

"Even if that is true, I shouldn't be stepping out on my boyfriend. Unhappy or not, he deserves for me to end things, not cheat on him." She touched my shoulder gently and walked around me.

"He's not making you happy and you're telling me what he deserves? Happy, I been around you a few times and I just want to make you happy."

"Daddy! I'm home!" River hollered soon as she came through the door. Whenever I was off from work, it was something she did.

"In your room, baby!" I yelled back and watched Happy take a seat in the chair that I had been sitting in.

We both stood there and listened to her stomp up the stairs. She walked into her room confused when she laid eyes on Happy. "Um, daddy, who is she?"

"This is my surprise for you."

"Surprise?"

"My friend is a stylist and she brought you some outfits to try o—"

"OMG! A real stylist!" she hollered and ran right over to Happy. "What did you bring for me? Is it pink or glitter stuff?" she bombarded her with questions.

Happy smiled. "I wouldn't be doing my job if I didn't add those things. Every girl has to have sparkle and pink."

"I like her already, daddy." River smiled and placed her little purse on her desk. Since she entered fifth grade, she couldn't just take her bookbag but had to have a little purse, too.

"I'm Happy Galleria." She extended her hand and River shook it.

"I love your name. My name is unique, too," she smiled.

"I love your name more than mine," Happy smiled. "If you're comfortable, me and you can try on some options and kick Dad out."

"Wait, what? Y'all gonna kick me out?"

"Uh.. yes, daddy. I need to find my birthday outfit." She smiled and pulled me by my arm, out the room. "Sit at the kitchen table with Granny and I'll come down to model for you both," she instructed and stood in the doorway. I saw Happy mouth sorry and laughed. River slammed the door and I could hear her starting to talk Happy's ear off.

When I got downstairs, my mother was pulling out the meat she had marinated the night before. When she saw me come down, she smiled. "Hey, baby boy. What is River up there hollering about now?"

"I got a stylist to come style her for her birthday."

"That was nice. You know she loves anything fashion. Is she upstairs?"

"Yeah, she brought the clothes by for River to try on." I took a seat at the kitchen island while she grabbed the fresh broccoli and then rice out the pantry.

"Can't believe she's going to be eleven in a few days. I went out and ordered her cake from Publix earlier when I went to get my hair done."

"Appreciate it." I smiled.

There was silence and I was looking down at my phone.

She talks a lot.. sorry.

She's fine. I love how passionate she is about her look. She has style lol

That's my angel.

I see. You've raised her well. But, if she calls me ma'am one more time.

Chill. She was raised well.

"Boy, why you looking down at your phone with a big smirk on your face? You don't hear me talking to you?" My mother pulled me from the next text message I was about to send.

"What happened?"

"Who you texting?"

"The stylist. I was seeing how long they were going to be up there."

My mother pursed her lips and stared at me. "Who you fooling, Colt?"

If there was one person I couldn't hide something from, it was my mother. She knew when I was blowing smoke up her ass. "I met her when I went on vacation. We met on the plane and then had dinner on the resort."

My mother abandoned the counter and came over to the table. "You didn't tell me that."

"Because I knew you would do this."

"Do what?"

"Ma, you ran from the counter to me like the devil was on your heels."

She swatted me and went back over to the counter. "Do you see this going anywhere?"

"I'm not sure."

"Well, I'm glad someone has you—"

"This is the first look." River came down with Happy behind her. She had on a gray sweatshirt that had an ice cream cone that sparkled, a pink tutu, and she wore sparkle leggings under with a pair of Doc Marten boots.

"I picked a bunch of options and she tried them all, but she paired two of the outfits together, and made this." Happy came down the rest of the stairs. "She has great style, I love it."

River modeled around the kitchen and flipped her hair a few times. "I love it, River," my mother said.

"Thanks, Granny. Milani is going to be so happy when she sees my outfit." She continued to flaunt around the kitchen like a supermodel. The smile on her face was unexplainable. All I knew was that it brought me so much joy to see my daughter this happy.

"Go upstairs and change clothes. Put it in my room so I can hang it up nicely in your closet. While you're up there, start on that homework before dinner," my mother told her and she smiled, then took off up the stairs.

Happy smiled and walked toward my mother. "How are you, Ms. Wright? My name is Happy Galleria." She extended her hand.

"Girl, I'm a hugger. Come give me a hug." My mother pulled her into a hug. Happy appeared to have melted in her arms. My mother's hugs had that effect on people. She was one of those people who you could sit and talk to and she wouldn't judge you for a thing that came out of your mouth.

"Aw, well, I love hugs." She laughed and stepped back. "I'll grab my purse and be on the way. Colt, she wants to keep all the options I grabbed, so I'll be sure to send you the bill." She winked at me and headed to the living room.

"No need to rush off. I'm cooking dinner and I would love to have you at my dining table tonight. Happy fixed her mouth to speak and my mother spoke over her. "And before you decline, I don't take too nice to people turning down some dinner from me."

"In that case, how could I decline?" Happy smiled.

"Ma, how you gonna bully her into staying for dinner? She don't have to stay if she doesn't want to."

"She said she's staying. It's final. Go on and show her your little man cave you never let any of us see."

"Ma, you clowning right now. You and River always down there watching my TV." I went over and hugged her.

"Yeah, yeah, yeah." She waved me off. "River is doing her homework and you guys can watch a movie or something. I'll call you up when supper is done," she told us and shooed us out the kitchen. I looked back as I led Happy down the stairs and my mother stood there smirking with her mixing spoon in her hand. This woman was going to drive me crazy.

Chapter Seven

ALL THAT IS ON MY MIND IS YOU

Happy

We sat on Colt's sectional and watched the news for twenty minutes. Neither of us said a thing. I was sitting on the opposite side from him with some space in between us. He had taken a business call for ten of the minutes. He tried to rush the person off the phone, but I told him to handle his business. His man cave was a typical man's room. He had a brown sectional couch that wrapped around and was faced in front of a seventy-five-inch flat screen which was mounted on the wall. He had a fridge, small mini bar and some collectibles sitting on a display case. Then in the corner, he had a desk with papers neatly stacked along with a computer and a comfortable computer chair. You could tell he was into being neat and didn't deal with clutter at all.

"My bad for taking long on the phone, and for getting all into the news like that. So much shit always happening and I like to know what's going on."

"I agree."

"Sorry about my mama. She thinks she can find me a wife by holding you hostage," he apologized.

"Don't act like you don't like it," I laughed.

"Now, I didn't say all of that."

"Exactly, you like me being in your presence."

"Indeed." He moved closer.

"Colt, you already know I'm in a situation."

He moved back slightly and stared at me. "Does he know you're in a situation?" I was a bit taken aback by his question. What he had asked was a good question to ask because lately, I didn't know what was up with Phil and me lately. He was working more and I was barely able to get him on the phone. Hell, I spoke to his assistant more than him and it was starting to bother me. "That wasn't fair." He backed away.

"I'm glad you realized that," I made sure to point out. He was right, still, it wasn't his place. Or maybe it wasn't my place to express how I felt to him about my boyfriend. Either way, I wasn't about to do this right now.

"And I'm sorry about that."

"Where's River's mother? Do you guys share custody or something?" I decided to switch the subject. I never heard him mention her the few times we had spoken. And, I was pretty sure if her mother was around, she would have been able to style her own child.

"She passed away when River turned five."

I gasped and held my hand over my mouth. "I'm so sorry, Colt. I didn't mea—"

He gently touched my arm. "You're fine. She died from cancer. River doesn't speak about her much because she doesn't remember that much about her."

"Were you guys together or...?"

"Yeah. We planned a whole future together." He clasped his hands together and looked straight ahead. "She fought so hard and then lost her battle."

"Is that why you moved to Georgia?"

"Part of the reason. I felt like I was drowning being in New York. I moved us to a new apartment and felt like everything about the city reminded me of her. I wanted — nah, I needed a new start."

I rubbed his shoulders and looked at the side of his face. I could tell River's mother meant a great deal to him by the way his emotions shifted and how his voice lowered when he mentioned her. This woman was probably the love of his life and he lost her in the worst way possible.

"I'm so sorry, Colt. It probably doesn't mean anything, but from meeting River today, you're doing an amazing job with her."

"Appreciate it. The older she gets, she looks just like her mother. And man, she act just like her, too."

"I can only imagine. Losing a mother at such a young age is hard, but both you and your mother have made up for it. You both can never replace her mother, and you both know that, but she's growing up with two wonderful people who wouldn't hesitate to give her the world."

"I really appreciate that." He finally turned and looked me in the eyes. We both stood there looking at each other. Leaning forward, I placed my lips onto his, then held the side of his face. He took both of his hands and cupped my face to kiss me deeply.

We broke the kiss and stared at each other. "I'm sorry."

"For what?"

"I don't want to give you mixed signals. I'm the first one screaming I have a boyfriend, then here I am, kissing you on the lips."

"You hear me complaining?"

"Not right now."

He took hold of the side of my face and brought me close to his face to kiss him. We continued to kiss each other, which led to me straddling him and continuing to kiss him. Not once did he try to rip my clothes off or try and have sex with me. Instead, he kept his hands around my waist as I held his face with my hands and our tongues continued to dance in each other's mouth.

"Daddy, Granny said she needs you to run and get some BBQ sauce." River yelled and we pulled away from the kiss. I went to move, and he held me in place.

"Nah, stay right here."

"Tell her to use Instacart," he replied.

"Okay."

"I should move."

"What about what I want?" He looked me in the eyes and made it impossible for me to avoid eye contact.

"Colt, I don't know anything about ordering food off Instagram. Boy, head to the store for me and tell Happy to come up and chat while you're gone."

"Can I have one more kiss before I head to the store?"

I leaned forward, my hair falling on his face, and kissed him again. "No more after today. We've done too much."

"Only if you agree to go out to dinner with me." I sat and debated for a second before I climbed off him. Even in the midst of me climbing off him, he kissed me one more time. "Lips so soft."

"I exfoliate them," I replied and fixed my dress. "Come on."

Leaving my purse, I headed upstairs where his mother was still in the kitchen cooking. Colt headed to the store and I sat at the kitchen island next to River.

"You're really pretty," River complimented.

"Aw, thank you!"

"Tell me about yourself, Happy." His mother turned from the oven and stared at me. I couldn't remember myself being this nervous when I met Phil's parents.

"I'm twenty-nine and I'm a stylist. My father owns Galleria stores and I worked as a stylist there for a few years before I decided to step out on faith and do it alone."

"What? I love those stores. People treat you real right in there. And your family owns them?"

"Yes, ma'am. My father started it when he was younger."

"Faith, huh? I know your father wasn't too pleased about that." She laughed and grabbed her dishcloth to wipe the counter down.

"He wasn't happy at all. I started a fashion blog a few years back and it took off, so I decided to use that platform to find my clientele."

"And my son? How do you feel about him?"

"You've raised an amazing man, Ms. Wright. He's so respectful and I love the passion he has for his career."

"When he told me that was what he wanted to do, I could have cried. I don't know why he like being up in that damn sky." She sucked her teeth. "He lost a lot of friends from our old neighborhood and he has some friends still wrapped up in them streets. I thank God for steering my baby the right way."

"You can definitely pat yourself on the back because he's a good man," I responded. "And you have an amazing daddy." I turned my attention to River, who had her nose in a book.

"Thank you." She giggled and returned her focus back to her book.

"Being completely honest with you, Ms. Wright... I have a boyfriend. Me and Colt are just friends."

"I see the way you look at my son. The way you stared at him when you and River first came down the stairs, I know you're feeling something for him."

I blushed because what she was saying was true. Colt made me feel something I hadn't felt in a long time. When he smiled, he made me want to smile, too. The way he kissed and handled my body downstairs, I hadn't been handled like that in so long. Phil was so consumed with his career I came second to that. When he did finally get around to me, the passion wasn't there anymore. It was as if he was doing me a favor by having dinner or having sex with me. It saddened me that this was what my relationship had come to.

"Ms. Wright, I promise we're friends. I'm very fond of your son, as a friend."

"Baby girl, tell that to your friends... I know what I saw. And, my silly ass son over here smirking at his phone like you sitting right in his face. I know what I see."

We sat and chatted for a few before Colt arrived back at the house. "Boy, I sent you for some sauce. What took you thirty minutes?" Ms. Wright snatched the sauce and went right to work, putting it over the chicken.

I was emailing a client back about our meeting, and texting Kharisma about our brunch plans that she had canceled. She promised she would be ready tomorrow. When I looked up, Colt was standing there with a dozen roses in his hands. Placing my phone on the counter, I smiled like a smitten fool.

"For me? You didn't have to do that." I stood up and accepted the flowers before hugging him.

"Aw, daddy... You're such a gentleman." River finally looked up from her book.

This man was making it hard to ignore his advances. First, the kiss, now flowers, then he planned to take me out to dinner. I was out here living like I didn't have a man I wanted a proposal from. Even still, I couldn't act like I wasn't loving the attention Colt was giving me.

"Again, thank you so much for these." I smelled them, then looked back up at him.

We sat in the kitchen and spoke while Ms. Wright finished up dinner. When she was done, Colt popped a fresh bottle of wine and we brought the conversation into the dining room. Everything about the conversation came so easy and wasn't forced. I didn't have to act properly or speak using big words like I did with Phil's parents. While I loved his parents, they didn't know how to just have a normal dinner. It was always so formal and I felt like I was going to suffocate. Not to mention, the elephant in the room between both Phil and his father. While Kendra, Phil's mother, wanted dinner to be an amazing experience, it never turned out like that. We sat there while our silverware hit the plates and did the talking for us. It felt nice to eat BBQ chicken, sip wine and have a conversation that didn't consist of my future.

. . .

"Girl, so you kissed him?" Kharisma nearly choked on the smoked salmon she had just taken a bite of.

"Khar, I straddled him." I slouched further in my chair when I thought about what had gone on earlier this week.

Kharisma had been busy with her practice and I had been busy with a picky client, so we decided to meet Saturday for brunch at our favorite restaurant here in the city. Kharisma sat across from me so tickled by what I had said to her.

"Lawd, you were trying to hand him the panties. What happened after?"

"His daughter broke it up because his mother needed him."

She put her Bloody Mary down and stared at me. "Wait, he lives with his mama?"

I rolled my eyes because I knew she would make a big deal out of it. "Correction, his mother lives with him. Since he works a lot, she lives there to help out with his daughter."

"That makes a lot of sense. What did his mother think of you?"

"She called me out about having feelings for her son. Told me she saw how I looked at her son. She basically called me the hell out."

"And is she right?" I sat up and busied myself with the shrimp and grits on my plate. "Happy Joy Galleria!" She lightly hit the table.

"I do like him. I feel bad about even feeling like that about him. Especially since I'm with Phil."

"Phil? Compared to Colt, are you crazy?"

"It's not about looks and you know that. Mom always says marriage is a business deal. It's about what a man can bring to the table."

"And you know that I don't agree with Mom's logic. Marriage should be about love and commitment, not about what someone can bring to the table."

Kharisma and Jade were dating two Blatimore brothers that

every girl in Atlanta wanted a piece of. The Blatimore family was well known in Savannah, Georgia. They were in the real estate business. From Savannah to Atlanta, Georgia, and everything in between, they were the brothers to see. Tommi Blatimore was the youngest and he and Kharisma had been together since her senior prom. Unlike me, Kharisma wasn't looking for an engagement ring, but she had gotten one. She and Tommi went to Dubai for a business trip, and he proposed to her on top of the Burj Khalifa. That was almost two years ago and she hadn't made any preparations for the wedding. We all asked and she simply brushed us off, telling us how busy both she and Tommi were.

"You're about to marry into a rich family, Khar. You don't need to worry about love or money because you have both with Tommi."

"And if he didn't have anything, I would still be with him."

"I can see the look on Mom's face now," I giggled.

My mother and Kharisma always butted heads because of many things. Kharisma was strong-willed and marched to the beat of her own drum. She did things because she felt moved to do them, not because someone wanted her to. Out of all of my mother's daughters, Kharisma was the one who gave her the most trouble. While my mother pushed us into our careers, me a stylist and Jade a wedding planner, she couldn't do the same with Kharisma. Kharisma wanted to be a doctor and let it be known when she graduated high school. She went away to college and my mother feared she and Tommi's relationship wouldn't stand the distance. All in all, my mother was worried about Kharisma being able to land and keep a Blatimore brother. And, because this was my mother's thought process, both she and Kharisma butted heads on the daily.

"You know she can't frown because of the Botox." She sipped the rest of her Bloody Mary. "I haven't spoken to Mom since your birthday dinner."

"Even then, the both of you didn't share more than three words. I know you've spoken to Dad plenty of times."

"Well, of course. He's my favorite. Dad doesn't judge and he isn't pushy with our lives."

"Only mine." I rolled my eyes.

"Even then, he was only consumed with the work you did for Galleria. Daddy never gets involved in you and Phil's relationship, it's more Mom."

She was right. It was my mother who called to check to see if I was doing my job as a girlfriend. For the first six months of our relationship, I would bring him a homemade lunch twice a week. It was hard trying to juggle my duties working for my father and be a good girlfriend. My mother told me this was how she landed my father and I needed to look at their marriage as a guide that I needed. My mother was born and raised in Columbus, Georgia. She was raised to be a wife; nothing more and nothing less. She was groomed to always look her best, never act beside herself, and always present herself as a lady. It was the reason my father called her his little Georgia peach. Out of the twenty-nine years in my life, I had never heard my mother raise her voice or act crazy. She was always poised, prim, and on top of her game. It was the reason she and my father had lasted all of these years together.

"True."

"Anyway, what's going to happen with Colt?"

"Nothing."

"What do you mean, nothing? He's obviously into you, Happy."

I pushed my plate away and stared into my sister's eyes. "He's into me and I'm into a relationship, Kharisma. Why do you keep forgetting that?"

Kharisma requested a refill of her drink and then turned her attention to me. "You've always done things Mom's way. Look where that got you. You weren't the least bit interested in Phil until Mom got in your ear."

Phil was a clean cut guy who came from a wealthy family. When I met him at a gala a few years ago, I wasn't intrigued because he spent the evening talking about himself. When it was time for me to talk, he would cut me off and tell me about an incident that happened in his life. My mother continued to keep pushing me over to him and we continued to talk. Eventually, that cocky behavior turned into a caring man who I grew to love. My mom was the one who pushed me into his arms, but it was Phil who sealed the deal.

"Phil is sweet, kind and car—"

"You don't need to convince me of that. Isn't your anniversary coming up?"

"Yeah, it's next week."

"Speaking of next week, are you going to Mom and Dad's for Thanksgiving dinner?"

"Yes, like I do every year. We may leave early to head to Phil's parents' after."

"I'll be in Savannah at Tommi's parents' estate." Kharisma broke the news to me. "And Jade is coming to this dinner, too."

I rolled my eyes because I knew she would bring her husband, Tony. Tony and I didn't get along and I didn't pretend to hide my distaste for the man. I hated that man's guts and wanted to puke up the food I had just consumed moments before.

"What is your dislike with Tony?"

"Nothing."

Kharisma saw my mood and decided to leave the subject alone. "It'll be nice for you and Jade to hang out. When is the last time we all sat down and hung out?"

"Never. She's either out of the country or up Tony's ass." I cut my eyes at Kharisma. Here she was trying to make it seem like hanging with Jade would be the highlight of Thanksgiving.

Jade was quiet, reserved, and the spitting image of my mother. The only exception was that she had a successful wedding planning business. My mother always said she had two jobs. One was to take care of her children and the other was my father. To my mother, a career was cute, but it wasn't needed when you married a man who had a career and money.

"Well, maybe you both should start hanging out. Did I tell you that me and Tommi are thinking about moving down to Savannah?"

My jaws dropped because I couldn't imagine not having my sister near. Savannah, Georgia, was almost four hours away from me. Whenever I needed my sister, that meant I had to climb into a car and head down there to spend time with her.

"No, you didn't tell me this."

"Well, Tommi's dad's health is failing so he needs to take a step back from the office there. You know that's the main office. Well, Tommi is thinking of moving down there and asked me what I think. Of course, he told me if I didn't want to move he wouldn't go."

"And you told him?"

"I told him I would think about it. I love the historic homes down there and I could easily open up another practice there and find another doctor to work at the one here."

"Forget the historic homes, Kharisma. You're going to move away because of your fiancé? He can grab a ride on Dad's helicopter."

"And so can you. You're acting like I'll be that far away. Either way, right now it's just talk because Tony is back in town and dealing with everything. Tommi knows his brother and knows he and Jade will be out the country as soon as he gets bored."

"When are they going to settle down? They've been married for three years and they still have that condo in Buckhead that they were living in before marriage."

Kharisma shrugged her shoulders. "I have no clue. When I do speak to Jade, she makes it seem like she's living her best life. Maybe they love traveling the world and acting like newlyweds."

"And her business... she ignores that, too."

Kharisma rolled her eyes. "Let Mom tell it, she plans them on the go and she has a bunch of staff underneath her who get the job done. It's one of the main reasons I haven't asked her to plan my wedding."

"She's your sister."

"So? I don't want her little minions planning my wedding. If I'm paying, which I know I will be, I want Jade Galleria-Blatimore planning my wedding."

Raising my wine glass before sipping, I replied, "You have a point." Jade made it known that just because we were family, she didn't give family discounts. "A very good point."

"I may be about to marry into more money, doesn't mean I don't want what I'm paying for. Besides all of that, I'm happy we finally got together to catch up."

"Me too. It was well needed. Can you believe the last time we've gotten together was our trip?"

"Adulting sucks," she giggled.

"I'll toast to that." We both raised our glasses and toasted to a successful brunch with just the both of us. It felt nice to sit and connect with my sister from time to time. She was busy and I was equally busy, so we both took whatever time we could with each other.

After Kharisma and I parted ways, I headed over to Phil's condo. Today was his day off, and if I knew Phil, he would be doing yoga with his instructor. Whenever I made fun of him about doing yoga, he got serious and scolded how it kept him calm. It had been a few days since I had seen my man and I wanted to love on him for a second. Part of me felt super guilty for the make-out session Colt and I shared. How could something so wrong feel all right? It was a question I found myself asking every time Colt's number came across my phone. Since we shared those kisses, we spoke on the phone and would FaceTime when either of us was available. His daughter's birthday went off without a hitch, and I was the first person she wanted to call to thank. She told me how everyone loved her outfit and she appreciated me for helping her pull a look together.

Colt was back to work and our conversations were limited because he had been flying out the country often. When he did have time to chat, I made sure to avoid that kiss. Meanwhile, Colt wanted to keep talking about the kisses we shared. I couldn't lie, whenever he called, my heart sped up and those little butterflies swirled around my stomach. It was a feeling I loved, but it was a feeling I should have been feeling toward my boyfriend, not Colt.

Using my key, I let myself into his condo and found him sitting on the couch. He had his laptop, papers and his phone glued to the side of his face. When he saw me, he smiled and held his finger up for me to wait a second. I had become so used to Phil having a phone to his ear, that seeing him without a phone next to his ear was shocking to me. I plopped down on the couch beside him as he finished up his conversation on the phone. From his tone and how urgent he sounded when demanding what he needed, I knew he was doing something for his boss. Since he knew that becoming partner was in his grasp, he had become obsessed with any and everything pertaining to his boss. I wanted just a small piece of the attention he gave his boss.

"Hey, baby, what brings you by?" He placed his phone down and kissed me on the lips. "Hmm, give me another one," he told me and I kissed him again.

"I was at brunch with Kharisma and decided to see what you were up to on your day off. Babe, I miss you."

He pulled me into his arms and kissed me on the neck. "I've missed you like no other. I can tell you this much, making partner is mine."

"Really? How do you know?"

"He was so pleased with the donation your father left at the gala. Six hundred thousand dollars, cash."

"Daddy loves giving back to charity. What does that have to do with you making partner?"

"Apparently, our firm has been trying to land your father as a client for a long time. His account would mean major money for the firm."

"My father has had his lawyer for years and would drop dead before he switches to a new one."

He rubbed my shoulders. "When we get married, he'll want to keep business in the family."

"Phil, I really don't want to talk about this. We're not married and you haven't made partner yet." I stood up. "I came over to spend time with you since we never get to do that anymore."

"I have some work to wrap up, then me and you can cuddle up on the balcony with hot cocoa and talk about your day," he suggested.

"Sounds like a plan. I'll go soak in the tub while you're finishing up work." I turned on my heels and headed to his bedroom.

Phil had a huge tub that was beautiful and you could get lost in. I always filled it to the top and dropped some lavender oil in the bath water. It was afternoon and I knew this oil would have me feeling sleepy. Cuddling on the balcony with some hot cocoa sounded like something right out of a Hallmark movie, and I'd be lying through my teeth if I said I didn't want to experience it.

Wheels up. Colt's name came across my screen. Whenever he was about to take off, he would send me a short message letting me know he would be up in the air, just in case I tried to call him.

Safe flight. Speak to you soon.

Bet.

I turned my phone off, placed it inside my purse and put my purse inside Phil's closet. Tonight, I didn't want any interruptions, just Phil and I, enjoying each other. It had been a while since we both got the chance to explore each other's body, and I *needed* this more than he knew. It was part of the reason I straddled Colt, and in any moment, if he decided to take it further than we did, I probably would have been ready and willing to go there with him.

Chapter Eight

DATING FOR A PURPOSE

Colt

I sat across the table from this woman I had met on Tinder. Darrius had talked me into making a profile. Happy had been consumed with her dude, so she and I didn't get up much. She sent me short messages letting me know she was fine and asked about my mother and River. Whenever I tried to go out with her, she told me she was doing dinner with her boyfriend. After trying to get her out, I decided to follow Darrius' advice and here I was, on a date with a teacher. We had spoken on the app for a few before she asked for my number. We spoke on the phone and she didn't sound like a loose chick, so I agreed to meet her for dinner. Everything about the date was going fine and I had no complaints. She spoke well, carried herself better, and she was a beautiful chocolate woman. Not to mention, she was a teacher and helped children. What more could I have asked for?

"So, he cries so loud and I'm standing there stuck with not a clue what to do." She giggled as I caught the tail end of her story.

"Dang, that's crazy." I laughed and drank my bourbon. "How did you get into teaching?" I questioned.

I see you. I received a message from Happy.

How?

She's pretty.

Where you at? I waited for another message and didn't receive one.

"Is everything fine?"

"I'm sorry, Azmina. My daughter always has to text me before she heads to bed," I quickly lied.

She smiled. "That's adorable. To answer your question, my mother worked as a teacher in Fulton County schools for thirty years. My father drove the buses for the same county, so it was in the cards for me to become a school teacher."

"Wow, that's amazing."

"Thank you. What made you want to become a pilot? I can't say I meet many black pilots," she admitted.

"If I had money for every time someone told me that. I've always been obsessed with planes as a child. It took a while to find my path, but I found it and always followed it."

"You wouldn't believe me, but I'm terrified of planes. I've only been on a plane once and it was to Miami for spring break during college."

"Nah, you serious?"

"So serious," she laughed.

"I gotta get you on a plane then. We can take a quick trip and I'll hold your hand the entire flight." She blushed and removed her hair from her face.

"I might have to take you up on that offer."

Bathroom.

"Can you excuse me real quick? I gotta use the bathroom," I quickly excused myself. By the time she replied, I was already out my seat and headed to the bathroom.

When I made it over to the bathroom, I saw Happy standing there. She was dressed in a tight red dress that hugged every curve of her body. Her curly tresses were straightened and pulled into an updo. When she laid eyes on me, she smiled and reached for a hug. As I hugged her, I couldn't help but take in her fruity scent. This woman always smelled good whenever I was around her.

"Hey, how are you?" She tried to be all professional and I cut all that shit.

Shoving her into the family bathroom, I locked the door behind us and pushed my lips onto hers. She wrapped her arms around my neck and I picked her up. Feeling her legs wrap around my body, I knew she wanted this – probably more than I did. Shoving my tongue down her throat, I pulled back to look into her eyes.

"What?" She looked at me, confused.

"You're so beautiful."

She kissed me on the lips and I leaned her against the wall while feeling her body. We broke our kiss and I let her back onto the floor. "We can't keep doing this."

"Why, because you're going to want more?"

"Being honest? Yes," she admitted.

"Why you haven't been calling me or answering your phone?"

"I've been busy." She was vague with her answer.

"Busy?"

"Me and Phil have been spending a lot of time together, so I haven't been able to be on my phone much," she replied honestly.

I couldn't stand here and act like her response didn't hurt a little bit. "I see."

"Don't do that. You're on a date with another woman, so you're clearly not home, worried about me."

"Yeah, because you weren't answering my phone calls. It's something small, so don't get all worried."

"Colt, I don't want you not taking dates seriously because of me. You deserve a good woman."

"My mother is on my ass about inviting you to Thanksgiving dinner. I'm off, but I fly out the next day."

"I would love to come, but I'll be over my parents' house for dinner."

"Nah, no problem. You're fine. Let me get back to my date." I unlocked the door and she touched my hand.

"Colt, don't be like this."

"You good, Happy. Enjoy the rest of your evening." I turned around and kissed her so hard before letting her go and leaving the bathroom.

When I got back to the table, Azmina was staring down at her cell phone. When she saw me come to the table, she offered a slight smile and placed her phone back into her purse.

"Sorry about that. This one man was talking my ear off about where I got my dress shoes from."

"Um, what? In the bathroom? I can't stand when people hold random conversations," she laughed. "I'm sorry you had to go through that."

"You don't know the half. I know a bar not too far from here, want to grab some drinks after dinner?"

"I hope your place has good wine. I'm a wine connoisseur."

I waved the waiter over for the check. "Oh, yeah? I definitely gotta take you to my favorite winery here in Georgia."

"Are you talking about the one in Braselton?"

"You've been?"

"Not yet. My friend has been trying to get me to their spa, but I've been busy with work and afterschool."

"I'm not too sure about the spa, but if you want some good wine, I would love to take you there," I offered. The date went well and I wouldn't mind having a second date with her.

Azmina was a good woman with her head on straight. Would I bring her over to meet my mother right away? Probably not. I didn't see a problem with having another date and seeing where this could go. My mind was on Happy and how we always came close to having sex, then we stopped. It wasn't like she didn't tell me she had a boyfriend ahead of time. Her boyfriend was all she ever mentioned. Still, I ignored the fact that she had a boyfriend because her actions showed me something different. Her actions showed me that if I were to make a move, her body would willingly accept it. There was no secret that Happy was giving me mixed signals. Even with all the mixed signals, I wanted her bad, like a crack head wanted his next hit.

I pulled up to Azmina's house and watched as she fumbled with her clutch to locate her house keys. We decided to skip the bar since she had work in the morning. I was due to fly out in the afternoon, and even then, I was just doing four flights back and forth to Miami. That was light work to me, so I wasn't concerned about staying out late. Both Darrius and I worked together, so it would be simple and cool flights back and forth.

"Um, would you like to come in for some wine?" She held up her key and smiled at me.

"Sure," I replied and killed the engine. Azmina lived in a starter home subdivision in Fulton County.

Seeing a woman own her own home, have a career, and have a nice Toyota parked in her driveway turned me on. When I was younger, I used to be attracted to women who had nothing going for them. Yeah, they had the nice body and could probably suck me dry, but what else did they have to offer? Azmina was a teacher, owned her own home, and had a lot going for her, other than looks.

"How long have you lived here? These houses are nice," I complimented as we walked up the driveway.

"About a year. I lived with my parents for a few years after college to save for a down payment. Soon as I was able, I took the leap and bought my own home," she explained as she pushed the key into the lock and unlocked the door.

She let me inside and I looked around her house. It was quaint and cozy. Her house was painted in earth tones with African statues placed throughout the house. I could smell vanilla the further I walked into her house. She set her purse on the kitchen counter, then went to the wine fridge that was in her cabinet.

"I respect it. My moms lives with me and it helps me out with my daughter."

"See, you understand. My friends were all ready to leave their parents' house and now all of them rent. My plan was to live with my parents until I met someone and eventually got married so we could buy our first home together... you know?"

"And how is that turning out?" I joked.

"Quit it," she smiled before rolling her eyes. I watched as she popped open a bottle of Alamos Cabernet Sauvignon 2013 and poured it into two wine glasses. "I thought by now I would have been married and moving into a home with my husband. Not a single, twenty-eight-year-old who spends her nights grading papers and falling asleep on her sofa."

"I didn't see myself on Tinder, looking for a date, either, if this is where you're heading," I chuckled.

She handed me the glass of wine and waved for me to follow her. We walked into her living room and sat on the couch. "That part, too. I used to make fun of my friends who dated online, and now look at me."

"I had nothing against it, just always thought it wasn't for me."

"Same here. Why do you think it's so hard trying to find someone? For me, men don't want to be committed, and when you speak of marriage, it's like they get turned off."

"And how many dates have you gone on that you mentioned marriage?"

She silently counted in her head, then took a sip of wine before she spoke. "A few."

"You gotta remember some men are on this date to just get a free fuck. They figure it's easier than going out to meet women the old way. If they're only looking to have sex, then marriage isn't on their radar. I'm dating with a purpose. I have a daughter and don't have time to play games with women. I want — no, I *need* a woman who wants me and understands what comes with loving me."

She looked up at her ceiling. "Good Lord, where have you been hiding this man?" We both shared a laugh. "All I want to know is that I'm not wasting my time. I've had a friend who dated this man for four years, had a baby and he told her she wasn't marriage material. Like, huh? She's good enough to bare your child, but not to carry your last name?"

"Damn, that's wild."

"Exactly. Then, they ended things and decided to just co-parent, and he goes and gets married a year later."

"What the hell?"

"My point exactly. She spent all those years expecting him to pop up and surprise her with the proposal of a lifetime and he never planned on doing it. This is why marriage should be a conversation during year one of dating. If you don't want to get married, then I have to exit stage left."

I noticed she spoke a lot of getting married. Like I told her, I was dating with purpose. I wasn't out here looking to have sex with a bunch of women and lay in my bed alone at the end of the night. As much as I was dating for a reason, I wasn't looking to rush into a marriage, either. I didn't believe in dating for a year and popping the question. A year was when the problems started to become real. Azmina seemed like she was looking for a man so she could rush him down the aisle.

"I feel you. You also have to take into account that men do things on their own time. You can't expect a man to tell you that he wants marriage right off the back, because some men don't want marriage until they meet the right woman."

She sipped her wine and stared at me through the corner of her eye. She had already refilled her drink and was about to refill it again. "Understandable. I just hate when men aren't upfront about their intentions. Let me know so I can move accordingly." She scooted closer to me and crossed her legs.

"This must be your favorite wine."

"It's so delicious. I pay only twenty bucks for this too at the liquor store. I'm on a teacher's salary." She guzzled the rest of her wine. I couldn't tell if she was a wine connoisseur or a wine-o.

She went from talking about having an early morning to

winking at me as she set her glass down. "I might need to pick me some up. It's not too bad. I'm more of a white wine guy."

As I spoke, her hands slid further and further down my jeans until she was touching my penis through my jeans. I was aroused because the dress she wore hugged all her curves, and when she bent over, the top of her breasts spilled out of the dress. Not to mention, I hadn't had sex in six months, so anybody feeling down there had me ready to break someone's headboard.

"I think someone likes me stroking his... ego," she chuckled and pulled at my jeans. I watched as she climbed down to the floor and positioned herself between my legs. She unbuckled my belt, pulled down my slacks and released my dick from my Calvin Klein boxers. "Uh-huh, he's really happy to see me." She winked and stroked it while staring into my eyes.

After a few strokes, I watched as her mouth widened and she took all of me into my mouth. I had been blessed between my legs, so seeing her cover the entire thing had my mind tripped out. She continued to suck up and down while staring right into my eyes. That poised and proper teacher at dinner wasn't the woman who was currently popping my dick out of her mouth.

"You see now why I'm marriage material?" She winked and went back to work. I leaned my head back and stared at her ceiling. If you would have told me that the date would have ended like this, I would have called you a liar.

The only sound that was being made was the sound of Azmina slurping and spitting on my dick. I closed my eyes and held her head in place because she had me about to curl my toes in a few. It was always the proper girls who turned out to be the biggest freaks. By now, I had enough of her mouth and I was ready to feel what she felt like on the inside. Digging into my pockets, I pulled out the one condom I carried around and held it up. She knew what I wanted and popped my dick out of her mouth and ripped the condom wrapper open with her teeth. I watched as she pushed it further and further down the shaft of my penis. When it was fully on, she hiked her dress up, pulled her thong to the side and straddled me on the couch. When she lowered herself down on me, I knew I was about to cause some trouble tonight. She might have been a teacher, but I was about to school her on what kind of dick game I put down.

I sat in my man cave watching the nightly news. It was two days before Thanksgiving and my mother was upstairs, finalizing her dinner menu. I didn't understand why she was cooking so much. It was only going to be three of us sitting down at the dining room table to give thanks. Not to mention, I was flying out early that next morning to Dubai. Part of me wanted to take a few days and spend some time, exploring the country. I had flown there a few times but never left my hotel room because I was usually flying right back out the next morning. Then I thought about my baby girl and knew I couldn't leave her again with my mother. My mother's sixtieth birthday was coming up and I had planned to send her on vacation for a week. She did everything and she deserved to be pampered on a beach while holding a drink.

Since having sex with Azmina, she had been blowing my phone up nearly every day. When she couldn't reach me, she would send me a bunch of messages and ask me to call her. The sex was incredible, and with what she held between her thighs, it was shocking that she wasn't snatched up with a ring on her finger. By morning, she had fucked and sucked me dry before she had to make her way to work. When we parted ways that morning, she was trying to make plans for dinner or going to the movies. I had to lie and tell her I had previous plans. The way she allowed the freak out when we crossed the threshold of her house turned me on but made me think how many other men she was doing the same thing to. It was something I laid in her bed thinking about while she laid on my chest, telling me how happy I made her.

It seemed like things didn't work out for Azmina because she wanted to rush into things. After one date, she was texting me about my plans for the holiday and trying to invite me over to her parents' house. I appreciated the offer and all, but I wasn't trying to meet her parents. It didn't matter if she introduced me as a friend, I didn't want to meet her parents and she wasn't going to meet my mother. Things like that took time, and when or if we ever got to that place, it would mean that much more. Azmina seemed like she was ready to meet River and have her calling her mommy. It was too quick and it freaked me out, so I had to step back from the situation.

I closed my eyes and put my head back while thinking about the week I'd had. Working was everything to me and I loved my career, still, it hurt when I couldn't really enjoy the holiday with my family. I had to eat and head right to sleep because, in the morning, I had hundreds of people depending on me to get them to their destination safely. It was something that allowed me to give my mother and daughter a life we didn't have growing up. My mother and I lived in the hood for most of my life, so being able to tell my mama she didn't have work again was a personal goal of mine. My phone started ringing, so I sighed and leaned up to grab the phone. The number that flashed on my screen wasn't recognizable, so I slid my finger across the screen and placed it to my ear.

"Hello?"

"What are you doing?" Happy's voice came through the line.

Leaning back with the phone to my ear, I kicked my feet up. "Sitting downstairs, watching the news."

"You're obsessed with the news."

"That may be true."

"Aren't you going to ask me what I'm doing?" she whined into the phone.

I smirked. "At nine at night, I can only imagine you're going to bed."

"Wrong."

"So what you doing?"

"Standing at your front door, afraid to knock because your mama might judge me."

"Quit fronting."

She laughed. "I'm serious. I drove all the way here and you're going to leave me here?"

"Go to the backyard," I instructed.

I now heard the wind in the background. "I'm here."

The basement had a door that led out to the backyard. I never used the door besides if I sat out there if I was in the mood for a cigar. When I opened the back door, she was standing over near the gate.

"Come on," I called and she quickly rushed over to me. For once, she wasn't decked out in the latest gear. She had on a Juicy Couture pink velour sweatsuit with a pair of beige UGGs. Her hair was still straightened and pulled into a sleek ponytail. Her face was bare, and for the first time, I realized she had freckles all over her face.

"Why are you staring at me?"

"I didn't know you had freckles."

"I pay good money on makeup to hide them." She giggled and welcomed herself into the basement.

"For what? They're beautiful," I complimented.

She took her leather jacket off and placed it on the back of the couch. "The kids in school used to make fun of them. They called them poop speckles, so as soon as I was able to wear makeup, I started to cover them."

I locked the door and walked back over to her. She stared up at me as I caressed her face. "Don't cover them anymore."

"Okay." She let a moan escape from between her lips.

"Nah, I need you to promise me."

"I can't promise you that. You don't want me to wear makeup?"

"Wear it, but don't cover your freckles, they look good. I like the natural you. No fancy clothes, heels, just you." I messed around with her hair. "Why you straighten it?"

"Phil likes when my hair is straightened," she admitted, then looked away.

"I figured," I replied and walked over to the mini fridge to grab us something to drink. "Why you changing yourself for a man? If a man can't accept you, then he's not the man for you."

"No water... I need something stronger." She plopped down on the couch.

"Oh, yeah? What's going on with you?"

"Today is my four-year anniversary with Phil, and he forgot. I called him, but he hasn't answered his phone," she sulked. "Four years, Colt. I cooked a huge meal, went out and bought lingerie and even went to the salon for them to go over my hair since my curls were starting to emerge. The least he could have done was remembered it was our anniversary and answered the phone." She continued to vent.

"Four years, huh?" I popped open the bottle of wine that Azmina had recommended. Before I tried this wine, I wasn't a big fan of red wine.

"Yes, and you would think I would have received a text or call all day. I spent the entire day ripping and running around Phipps Plaza and Lennox Square for a client in heels. Do you know how much pain my feet were in? And, the one thing I looked forward to was a call or something."

I passed her a glass of wine and sat down beside her. Sitting my glass on the coffee table, I took her foot into my lap and pulled her boot off. She had on pink lace socks and I slid those off her feet. She had to be a size five in women because my hand swallowed her entire foot.

"I can imagine," I replied and started rubbing her feet as she sipped her wine. "What made you come here?"

She shrugged her shoulders. "After the night we ran into each other at the restaurant, I felt like I needed to see you."

"You didn't think a call would suffice?"

Nodding, she stared at me. "I didn't. I think me and you do better with talking in person."

Happy and I were in this weird-ass space and I didn't know how to fix it. She knew I wanted her and still, she came around and let me kiss, rub and flirt with her. When it got too hot, then she brought up the fact that she had a boyfriend. Like now, she should have been driving around Atlanta in her Tesla, looking for her man, and she was sitting in my basement while I rubbed on her feet.

"You think so, huh?"

She tossed her head back and enjoyed her wine as I pulled her other boot off and started to massage both her feet at the same time. "I can't remember the last time I had a foot massage." I remained silent. "What's on your mind?"

"Nothing. Just want to know where I fit in your life. Am I the side nigga, or the friend who makes you feel good when your man is making you feel bad?"

She removed her feet from my hands and sat up to place her empty wine glass next to my full glass. "Why do you feel like that?"

"Because when shit is good with you and him, I don't hear from you. Let him fuck up, like today, and then you randomly pop up at my house."

"I don't have many friends, besides my sister. Although what we have is fresh, I consider you a friend."

"Friends don't want to fuck each other."

She sighed and looked down at her hands. "What do you want me to say? That you, a man I met a month ago, has me rethinking my relationship of four years? That whenever I'm around you, I'm thinking of the next time I get to be wrapped in your arms? How your home feels more like home than my own house. How can I say those things and not complicate us?"

"Happy, we're already complicated. I have feelings for you and those shits are deep. I want to be with you and give you the world. I want to make you feel like your name: Happy. I want to give you long dick until you cry. I can tell you haven't been handled, touched or fucked how you deserve to be."

I watched out of the corner of my eye as she squeezed her legs together. Happy knew she wanted me and she wanted to feel this. I stood up and grabbed at her sweats. She leaned back and allowed me to pull them down to her ankles, then pull them off. She wore a satin pair of pink panties. I bent down in front of her, opened her legs and pulled them down with my teeth. My lips brushed across her skin and sent shutters through her soul. Her eyes were closed and she allowed small moans to escape her mouth. Tossing the panties to the side, I parted her second set of lips with my tongue and pulled her legs further apart. I stuck my tongue deeper and deeper inside her as I listened to her whine in ecstasy. I lapped up her wetness like a cat did milk while inserting two fingers inside of her. My fingers matched the motion of my tongue. Happy held her ankles and moaned loudly. It didn't matter. The basement was soundproof, so if my mother was still awake, she wouldn't hear me.

"Stand up," I demanded.

She didn't hesitate. On shaky legs, she stood up and I spun her around and pushed her down. Palming her ass, I spread her butt cheeks and flicked my tongue in her booty. She wiggled while moaning.

"Coltttt, nooo... I never ha—"

"What I said?" I replied and she turned back around and arched her back further up.

I ate her from the back as she screamed out in pleasure. I positioned my body underneath her like she was a car and I was checking under the hood. Licking her from front to back, she collapsed on my face. I felt her moving her hips and riding my face. I sucked her pussy so hard, I was sure she would have hickies all across it. Happy held onto the couch and shook while gripping the couch. My mouth caught all the Happy juices she released into my mouth. While she was getting herself composed, I pulled my sweats down and released my dick. I picked her up and moved her from my face to my dick. I sat her down slowly as she gasped, feeling my width and length. I hated to bring God into this, however, He had blessed me down below.

"Oww, it hurts, Colt," she whined and I held her hips.

"Ride it," I demanded and she laid her head in the crook of my neck. She bit my neck as she started rotating her hips and riding me. "Still hurt?"

"Uh-huh, it's too much," she complained but didn't move. Phil must have been toting around a baby dick because she was acting like a virgin teen on her prom night.

Grabbing hold of her hips, I moved her up and down on my penis. She removed her face from my neck and stared into my eyes. Happy Galleria was so damn beautiful that it hurt. Everything about her made me want to try and give her the world. The way she needed me to take control in this moment and the small passion-filled moans she constantly did in my ear told me that she was lacking this at home, and needed this more than anything else in the world.

"Kiss me," she moaned.

With one hand, I took her face and stuck my tongue into her mouth. While she rode my dick, we kissed and were in our own moment. We fucked until three in the morning. I wanted to take my time exploring her body. With Happy, I didn't know when I would get another chance at this. When we both came and were satisfied, I guzzled my wine and carried her upstairs to my bedroom. My mother and River's room were upstairs and I had the master suite on the main floor. It was one of the reasons I was sold on this house. My mother and I could both have master bedrooms.

We laid in bed and Happy was cuddled in my arms. She rubbed my chest and kept placing small, wet kisses on me. "Is it serious?" She broke our silence.

"What you mean?"

"The woman you were on a date with... is it serious?"

"Nah, me and her went on a date, had sex, and we haven't seen each other since."

She lifted her head and stared at me. "Did you have sex with her like you did me?"

"Nah. You're special, and I already told you that."

She laid back down. "It would be selfish of me to feel jealous if you decided to continue to pursue something with that woman."

"It would be very selfish."

"I know it's selfish. It doesn't help that I feel like that."

I kissed her forehead. "Now you know how I feel about you and ol' dude."

She kissed my chest, then straddled me with half of her hair covering her face. "More," she demanded.

Her words were all I needed to get it back up again. "You feel him?"

"I do." She bent down and kissed me on the lips before lowering herself back onto my dick.

Chapter Nine

I REMEMBER

Happy

"When did you get a dog?" Jade walked into my townhouse with her fur coat, Birkin purse and dark shades over her eyes. She looked around and nodded in approval. "I see you used the interior decorator I suggested," she added.

It was Thanksgiving and Jade was back in the country to spend time with us for the holidays. When she called this morning, I started to ignore the call. Kharisma's voice was in my head, so I ended up answering the call. Jade was the best at everything growing up. Sports, cheer, school and everything above. In our private school, she was the most popular and everyone wanted to be like Jade. Even as an adult, she was popular and envied in our social groups. Everyone wanted to be Jade since she had married a Blatimore, had her own business and traveled the world.

"Phil forgot our anniversary and had someone bring this over the next day," I nonchalantly replied as I walked into my bedroom to put the finishing touches on my makeup.

"Your anniversary? Are you kidding me? I know you didn't let this little fleabag sway your decision in forgiving him?" She sounded horrified.

Looking at her, I walked into my bathroom. "No, he's still in the doghouse. No pun intended. He's been trying to see me and I haven't answered his calls," I yelled from the bathroom as I put another coat of lipstick on.

When I was done, I looked myself over in the mirror and headed back into my bedroom. Jade was sitting on my chaise lounge, petting the dog. "Good. Where are both of you going? Four years Mom told me. You should have something by now."

"This is something I'm trying to figure out, too," I lied. Since Colt had come into my life, the need to be married was becoming a little less important. I hadn't mentioned it to Phil in a while, and it felt nice not having to argue about his reasoning for not settling down right now.

"Do you want Tony to talk to him?"

"Nope."

"You need to hurry and finish your makeup," she sighed and decided to switch subjects. "You know Mama doesn't like us to arrive late to dinner."

"What do you mean? I'm done."

"Happy, you don't wear your freckles out... ever," she laughed. "And I don't know why. I wished I was blessed with some freckles."

"I've decided to go light on my makeup and show my freckles," I explained.

She stood up and smiled. "Well, good. I actually like when you show your freckles," she explained. "Anyway, I came over so we can drive over to Mommy and Daddy's together."

"You drove?" I laughed as I picked up my puppy and placed him in the Louis Vuitton dog bag he had come with.

"Oh, hell no... you know Georgia traffic is horrible. I have a driver outside..." Her voice trailed off. "You're bringing it?" She looked at the dog resting peacefully in the carrier.

"It's a he and his name is Brownie," I spoke of my chocolate covered Yorkie. He reminded me of a little piece of brownie.

I was pissed with Phil about missing our anniversary and in love with the gift he had decided to send a day late. A puppy was something I didn't think I needed, and having him in the house brightened me up. He followed me everywhere I walked and yapped at me when he couldn't get on the couch with me. It was the cutest thing ever, and it made me wonder if having a child felt somewhat similar.

"Well, you know Mama can't stand animals. Is he trained?"

"We're still finding out things about each other," I laughed.

"Clearly. Well, don't let him poop in the bag," she chuckled as we headed out the door. I set my alarm and closed the door behind me.

We were twenty minutes into the ride to my parents' mansion in Berkeley Lake, Georgia. My parents had owned our family estate for years. I remember growing up and playing on the circular staircase while my nannies chased me around. I also remember standing on those same steps when I went to prom and then graduated from high school. I've had good and bad memories in that house. The bad memories were part of the reason I rarely went over to visit.

"So, what's new with you besides Phil being a dick?" Jade finished tapping away at her phone and stared at me. Something seemed off with my sister. She was always snotty, judgmental and wasn't a pleasure to be around. Here she was, being almost the complete opposite of her regular self.

"I've spoken about me too much. What is new with you and Tony?" I tried hard not to choke his name out.

I was hesitant to mention Colt and what we had going on. Never in my twenty-nine years of life had I ever had sex the way he had sex with me. He was aggressive, yet gentle at the same time. The way he demanded me to fuck him and then kissed me on the lips had me turned on in the back of this car. Colt knew his way around a woman's body and knew the blessing that he carried between his legs. I was so embarrassed the next morning when I had to do the walk of shame out of his house. His mother and daughter were happy to see me, and I was mortified. My feelings for this man were real and I tried hard to hide them because I knew I was in a relationship with someone else. That night, we both crossed the line, and even as I sat here, I couldn't utter the word regret because I didn't regret anything we had done.

"Me and Tony have been good. He was having an affair when we were in Thailand," she admitted.

"An affair? How did you find out?"

"I found the keycard to the hotel he had her at. When I approached him, he didn't deny it and told me to stay in a wife's place."

"And what did you do?"

"I stayed in a wife's place." She hung her head, embarrassed.

I couldn't believe she had admitted that out loud. Even if that were the case, I would have lied and said I beat him or something similar. I wouldn't have been able to admit what she just had to anyone other than myself in private.

"Is he still seeing the woman?"

She grabbed some tissue from the center console and dabbed her eyes. "Yes, he says that he's in love with both of us and we can make this work. I'm sharing my husband with another woman."

I gently rubbed her shoulder and sighed. Jade got on both my and Kharisma's nerves and we talked mess about her behind her back, but at the end of the day, she was our sister and we loved her and wanted the best for her.

"Have you met the other woman?"

"No. He answers the phone right in front of me. Like, he doesn't even try to hide the fact that he's having an affair."

"Does Mama know?"

"Yes. She told me that I could either stick it out and continue to be married or I could file for divorce. She also mentioned my prenuptial agreement."

"You signed one of those?"

"Yes. If you would have come to our wedding, you would have

probably been in the room when I signed my life away." She tried to laugh to keep from shedding more tears.

"What were the terms of the agreement?" I hated Jade's husband, so anything that had to do with them getting married, I tuned out. I refused to attend or be a part of her wedding, and I forbid my parents to even speak about Jade and her husband to me. A good year into Jade's marriage was when I started talking to my sister again. Our relationship was very strained, and I was partly to blame for that.

"After seven years of marriage, if I decided to leave, I'd leave with three million dollars. If I decided to leave before the seven years, I didn't get anything."

"Jade, we come from money. Not to mention, your business makes great money. You don't need the Blatimore money."

"Do you see how Mama looks at me? Or better yet, Daddy? Do you see the sparkle in his eyes when he speaks about how successful I am, and how in love I am with my husband? He brags to all his business partners about the wealth I married into. My friends... they envy that my black ass married Tony." She sniffled and wiped her nose. "All those white girls we went to school with thought they had an advantage over me. They thought the Blatimore brothers wanted a white woman, and look at us. Me and Kharisma have two of the richest brothers in all of Georgia."

"Who cares what they think? Life is too short to not be happy."

"Happy, Mama may have named you Happy Joy Galleria, but you're not exactly happy with your life. Four years with Phil and all you have to show is a dog he couldn't hand deliver to you."

"I may not be the happiest right now, but I know eventually, I'll stop doing what everyone wants me to do."

"Everyone? You mean Mama? My husband didn't even propose to me because he was in love with me and wanted me to carry his last name. He proposed because of our meddling mama."

"I never knew that."

"Me either. Well, until Tony screamed it out during an argument." She chuckled and removed her hair out of her face.

"That's horrible."

"Ten minutes ETA, Mrs. Blatimore," the driver announced to Jade.

"Thank you, Roe," she replied and turned her attention back to me. "It's sad, but it's my life. I have to put on a smile and act like the happiest wife ever."

"Why don't you call me or Kharisma?"

"You and Kharisma have always been closest out of all of us. Not to mention, I know you both can't stand me or my husband. Why would I call to bother you with my problems?"

"Because we're your sisters. We can't stand how you act so high and mighty but we always want the best for you, Jade. It doesn't matter how I feel about you or your husband, I care and love you."

"I love you, too, Happy. Be unapologetically happy. Don't do anything for anyone except yourself," she advised.

"I receive that."

We pulled into the circular driveway and waited until the driver got out to open our doors. I held onto Brownie's carrier and climbed out of the car. Like my mother, she was waiting right near one of the six pillars that stood in front of the house.

"What is in that bag, Happy?" she hollered as she held her jacket closed.

"My puppy," I replied as I climbed the stairs in front of the house. "Phil got me a puppy."

"The man is a fool," she sighed. "He gets you a puppy and not a damn ring," she complained as she kissed me on both my cheeks.

"A complete fool," Jade added. "Hey, mama." She hugged and double kissed my mother on the cheeks.

"I have to talk with that man." She sucked her teeth. "Anywho, go and give that to Franchsia to keep watch over." She referred to one of the housekeepers. "Jade, my beautiful Jade." She stepped back and took her in.

I left them to their greetings and found Franchsia. She was

fluffing the pillows in the guest room downstairs. "Hey, Fran. Mama said for you to keep watch of my puppy during dinner."

"No problem. It's good seeing you, Happy. How are you?"

"Thank you. You too, I'm doing good," I smiled.

Unlike my mother, who believed we shouldn't be helping the help, I loved chatting with them. They were people with lives and had probably lived more than I did. People assumed because you grew up wealthy, you had probably lived life to the fullest. It wasn't true. I found people who didn't grow up as privileged than I did live much better. Like Colt, he got to live in Tokyo for a few years. My mother would have had a cow if I even suggested moving out of Georgia and to a foreign country.

"Thank you so much for pulling some outfits for my photo-shoot. I didn't know what I was doing." She laughed and walked toward me. She reached in her apron and pulled out an envelope. "Here's the money I owe you."

"Fran, I didn't do what I did for payment. You help my parents out a lot, and I appreciate you for it."

She was in the process of opening her own cleaning service. A lot of the housekeepers complained about the agency they worked for and how they paid them low and didn't offer benefits. Franchsia was opening up her own business, so I was honored that she had emailed me and asked me to help her out. I didn't do it for the monetary gain.

"I appreciate you. And, I'll have fun watching over this little one." She grabbed the bag out of my hand.

I found my mother and sister in the kitchen, micromanaging the staff. My mother never was one to lift her finger to cook, but she was always there to complain about something she didn't like. The same staff had been preparing Thanksgiving dinner since I was six. The food was always delicious and no one ever complained, so I didn't see the need for her to be so overbearing with them.

"Where's Daddy?"

"He's heading here now. Can you believe he had to go into the office this morning? The staff he has is so incompetent. You should have never left, baby girl."

"Daddy should have wanted to change."

"The Galleria brand is known for what we're known for. We can't allow you to go in and give our longtime clients heart attacks."

"Mama, I'm not trying to do that. All I want is for Daddy to allow me to pull together a line. It can be the Happy G. line and you'll see how much people want something new and fresh from the Galleria stores." I could tell from her eyes rolled in the back of her head that she didn't want to hear my pitch. She was always on my father's side, and I understood, she was his wife.

"Happy, why don't you pitch it to another designer? Your blog is huge and I'm sure someone wouldn't mind giving you a try. Cardi B just had a line with Fashion Nova. The pieces were nice, however, I know you can come harder."

"She will not go against the Galleria name. Enough of this talk before your father comes in and hears this." My mother turned around and sauntered out of the kitchen.

Jade and I both rolled our eyes at the same time and then laughed. "Seriously, I know a few clients in the fashion industry who have planned their weddings with me. I'll pull some names and let you work your magic," she informed me.

"Really? Jade, do you know how much that would mean to me?"

"Baby sis, I only want you to follow your dreams. I'll be flying back out tomorrow night. Tony has business in Singapore. We'll be there for a few weeks, but when I get back, I have a bunch of engagements with the business that will be among Atlanta's elite. Style me, and you'll be able to get your name out there."

"Really? I appreciate that, Jade." I hugged her. We shared our hug, then went to find my mother, who was complaining about the wine they had chosen to serve for dinner.

My dad had finally arrived and he was with Phil. I rolled my eyes when Phil smiled and hugged me tightly in front of my parents. My mother ate this mess up and I was sick to my stomach. Phil loved to come in and act like the doting boyfriend when he wasn't. He smelled like perfume and he wasn't around me, so whose perfume was it that I was smelling?

"I missed you, Angel." He kissed me on the forehead. "I need to talk to my love really quick." He pulled me into my father's study and slid the door closed.

"Phil, what are you doing here?"

"I called your father and told him that I messed up. He suggested that I show my face to dinner to make it right."

"Why in the world would you call my father? He has nothing to do with our relationship."

"I'm sure you went to talk to your mother about it."

"Uh, no. I didn't talk to anyone because I'm grown and don't need Mommy's advice."

He walked over to me and touched my hands. "I'm sorry, babe. I really messed up and there's nothing I can do to make it up to you." He tried to give an apology that would have meant something in the past. Now, it meant nothing to me.

"I'm tired, Phil."

"Let's grab doggy bags and then head to my place."

"No, I'm tired of you. I'm tired of whatever this is we're doing. I'm sick of it." I walked toward the window and looked out.

"Baby, I want to make this up to you. You know you mean the world to me. I'm just trying to give us a better life."

"Us a better life? I live a beautiful life. What's a better life when my boyfriend is never around for important things in our relationship? I'm alone in this relationship, Phil."

"I'm here."

"For how long? Right now isn't the time to talk about this. It's Thanksgiving and I'm here to spend time with my family."

He kissed me on the forehead. "We'll talk about it later. Just know I love you. How did you like your anniversary gift?"

"You bypassed every gift and got me a dog. Fitting." I chuckled and left him in my father's study. As soon as I turned the corner, I bumped right into Tony.

My body froze and the disgust was written all over my face. "Happy, what's going on? How are you?" He tried to make small talk.

I bypassed him and found my family in the dining room. Everyone was being seated. I sat next to my father, who sat at the head of the table, and across from my mother, who sat on his right. Jade sat next to the head of the table on the other side, and Tony filed into the room and took his seat. Phil sat next to my mother, across from me. A few of our family members filled the other seats. My Aunt Patty and Uncle Chuck had come from North Carolina to have dinner with us like they did every year. The kitchen staff came out of the room and started plating our food. My father was never one to carve the turkey like other families. He allowed the staff to carve the turkey and place it on the plate for us. Vomit tickled the back of my throat when I made eye contact with Tony.

"I'm thankful to have all of you sitting around this table with me. The only person I'm missing is Kharisma," he smiled.

"She could have spent the holiday with us." My mother made sure to make a snide remark about my sister.

"She's being a good fiancée. Isn't that what you wanted from us?"

"Happy, your tone," my father scolded.

"Sorry, daddy," I apologized and took a sip of my wine.

"Now, Kharisma is about to get married and she'll have to split her time between us and her new family. Tony is here and not with his family, so they switched spots." My father let out a hearty chuckle.

"He should have had dinner with the devil," I mumbled.

"You said something, Happy?" he had the nerve to ask.

His arrogance was a turn-off. The way he walked around like he was God's gift to earth pissed me off. This man was nothing except the devil in human form. I hated him and he knew I hated him, still, he continued to poke at me.

"I said that you should go to he—"

"Babe, what is wrong with you?" Phil interrupted what I was about to tell Tony's ass. He had some nerve to ask me what was wrong. He was part of what was wrong with me. Why did I continue to choose men who wasted my time?

"Happy, is something going on? You've hated Tony for years. I thought it was because he married your big sister and took her away. You need to deal with your issues and leave them at the door."

"Let's stop talking about this right now. Happy, you need to straighten up. Phil hasn't given you a ring because of this behavior."

"*My* behavior is why he hasn't proposed to me?" I laughed. "Way to instill confidence into your daughter, mom."

"Mrs. Galleria, I want to marry your daughter, I just want to make partner first. She deserves more."

"Boy, if you don't take that tired-ass excuse and shove it," I blurted. You ever thought something in your head and it came right out of your mouth? That was what had just happened and everyone stared at me with a shocked expression on their faces.

"Happy Joy Galleria!" My mother hit the table and raised her voice. "I get you're going through this identity crisis, and we've supported you during it. However, I won't tolerate the disrespect you're spewing from your lips."

"Hap, maybe you should take a walk and cool off." Tony had the nerve to open his mouth.

"Ton, maybe you shouldn't rape your wife's little sister on her prom night!" I slammed my hands on the table, stood up, and screamed.

Everyone's mouths dropped. Jade's mouth was moving, but nothing was coming out of it. "Happy, you're throwing around serious accusations here." My father pushed his plate away and stared at me. "Rape, Happy?"

Tears fell down my cheeks as flashbacks of what happened to me came rushing back. For years, I tried to bury what happened and move on, and just one look at him, it all came rushing back.

"This sick fuck raped me!" I continued to holler. The staff's mouths dropped as they looked on at the Tyler Perry drama that unfolded right in front of their eyes.

"Woah, woah... Rape?" Tony tried to act surprised.

"Happy, why didn't you tell anyone if this happened?" my father questioned.

I wiped back the tears and stared at my mother. "I did. I told Mama and she told me to keep my mouth shut. She told me that it was the slutty dress I wore and that I needed to keep quiet because Jade's future depended on it." I sobbed as I recounted everything that happened.

"You were dressed like a goddamn slut. A prom dress? That dress was something a damn hooker wears on a night stroll." My mom jumped up and decided to break the silence. "You've always been damn jealous of Jade, and I refused for you to lie and ruin her future with Tony."

My father sat back, looking in disbelief. "He took my virginity in mama's champagne room. All I wanted was a ride home from prom, and I got my hymen broke by force," I cried.

Pushing my chair back, I ran out of the dining room and found Franchsia. She was playing with Brownie and giggling as he licked her face. When she saw me enter the room, she noticed my disheveled appearance.

"Are you all right, Happy?"

"I just need Brownie," I sobbed.

She quickly handed me him and his bag, then looked at me. "I'm off. I was staying late to watch Brownie for you. You shouldn't drive like this, let me drive you home."

I arrived with Jade and her driver, so I had no other choice. "Okay. I'm not going home."

"Where? I'll drop you wherever." She pulled me into a hug.

"Lawrenceville."

"What's in Lawrenceville?" she asked, confused.

"Comfort."

Chapter Ten

DO YOU WANT TO?

Colt

When Happy arrived at my front door with red eyes and a wet face, I was furious. Who made her cry? Better yet, who made her unhappy? She had come with a Spanish woman who told me that she just wanted to make sure she got to her destination safely. I welcomed her into the house where my mother and River were in the living room, playing Monopoly. Happy was so irate she couldn't form three sentences to tell me what was wrong. It was a team effort when she crossed over our threshold. River grabbed the dog, my mother put some water on the stove for tea, and I pulled her onto my lap and kissed her on the neck. She didn't want to speak, and instead, she sobbed into my neck. She sipped some tea and then fell asleep in my arms. I carried her into my bedroom and laid her down. Closing the door behind me, I found my mother sitting at the kitchen island.

"Daddy, this dog is so cute." River giggled as she played with the playful puppy.

"Be careful with him, River," I informed her and sat down next to my mom.

My mom took a sip from her tea before she spoke. "Clearly this isn't just a friend situation here, Colt."

"I know."

"She has a boyfriend and came here for you. The way she cuddled into your arms for love and assurance, she has feelings for you, baby boy."

"And I have feelings for her, too."

"What happened to that child?"

"I don't know. I'm hoping she broke up with her man." If I was being completely honest, I didn't like Phil before I even knew his name. When I saw how beautiful Happy was and everything she brought to the table, I was jealous. I was jealous that a man other than me got to enjoy such a woman as herself.

"Colt!" my mom laughed.

"What? I just want to make her happy, Ma."

"I've never seen you like this about a girl." She shook her head. "Reminds me of when you and Tamia got together." She smiled. "It's nice seeing you care about someone other than me and River."

"I really care about her, mama."

"I can see that. You need to go and get some sleep. I hate when you're not well rested for your flight." She pulled the mom card out on me.

"I will. Love you." I kissed her on the cheek and went into the living room where River was playing with the dog.

"Dad, you need to get to sleep."

"Dang, you pulling the bedtime card on me?" I laughed and took a seat next to her. "You know I'm gonna miss you, right?"

"I know. And, I'm gonna miss you, too." She kissed me on the cheek. "I love you so much."

"Impossible."

She screwed her face up. "How you figure?"

"Because I love you ten times more than you think you love me," I countered.

"Fine." She gave up early on the game we loved to play. "Only because you have to work."

"I appreciate you, baby girl. Guess which river is my favorite river in the entire world?"

She put her finger to her chin and faked like she was thinking. "I'm not sure."

"River Wright." I pulled her and the dog into my arms and kissed her on the cheek. She giggled.

"Is everything all right with Miss Happy?"

"Everything will be fine, baby. I'll tell her you were worried about her."

"Thank you," she smiled.

"Don't stay up too late." I kissed her on the forehead, then headed down the hall to my bedroom.

When I opened the door, Happy was sitting in the middle of the bed with her cell phone in her hand. "It won't stop ringing," she complained. "I just want to sleep."

"Give it to me."

She handed me the phone and I powered it off. "There."

"Thank you," she sniffled. "For everything."

I sat down on the side of the bed and stared at her. "Are you going to tell me what happened?"

"Not right now," she whispered. "I don't want to think about it."

"I hear you, but will you ever tell me what happened?"

She touched my arm. "I promise I will tell you. Just not tonight."

"You've never done anything spontaneous, have you?" She shook her head no. "Come with me to Dubai."

"Dubai?" she choked out.

"I have to fly there tomorrow. Since it's a long flight, it's mandatory that we take a day break. I was going to use two extra days for vacation and we can spend time together to see the city."

"Okay."

"Seriously?"

"I need to get away. If that means getting away to Dubai with you, then I'm so down." She offered a weak smile.

I grabbed her face and placed a kiss on her lips. She allowed me to give her small pecks on her lips. "Happy, you don't realize how you make me feel."

"Explain it to me," she whispered.

"You make me feel like Tamia placed you in my path for a second chance at love. I feel like nothing can stop me, like I'm invincible. When you're not with me, you're on my mind."

"I want you bad, Colt Wright."

"Then have me, Happy Galleria."

She shook back tears. "It's too complicated. My family, Phil and his parents, there's too many people involved."

"Too many people involved in your happiness. Why are you doing what everyone else wants? You have something real right here. Why are you so scared?"

"I'm scared of giving up what I know for something so unfamiliar. You're like nothing I've ever experienced, Colt," she finally admitted. "If you were to break my heart, I don't think I could move forward."

"Why do you think I would hurt you?" I held her in my arms.

"You're too good to be true. I feel like the other shoe is going to drop. Nothing good like this ever happens in my life."

"Have you prayed for something good to happen in your life?"

"Every single night."

"Maybe He's finally ready to give you what you've been praying for."

She leaned up and stared me in the eyes. "I'm twenty-nine and never had anything to be responsible for. I mean, I just got a dog that I'm struggling with trying to keep alive. You're in your thirties, a father, and you have a career you love. I'm working off a few clients, writing a blog with a bowl of cereal in the morning while paying my bills with my savings. I walk around like my life is every bit of together and the truth is, It's not."

"I'm in my thirties and I haven't had a serious relationship since my daughter's mother passed away. I spend my days working because I feel guilty and want to give my mother and daughter the world."

"Guilty? Colt, why do you feel guilty?" She touched the side of my face.

"Tamia passing away. I feel like that shit was on me. I know that I couldn't have gave her cancer, but when she passed and left my daughter without a mother, I took that guilt. My mother wants more grandchildren and to see me happy with a wife."

"A mother's love is strong, and if Tamia had a choice, she would have never left her baby girl in this cold world without a mother. You can't hold the burden of guilt for what others want for you. Your mother wants to see you happy, even if it doesn't come with more grandchildren or a wife. You gotta stop holding that in," she explained and leaned up to kiss me on the lips.

"Just when the walls felt like they were closing in on me, I bumped into you. It was as if God or Tamia knew I needed you, Happy. If you chose to walk away, that shit would hurt more than you know."

She wrapped her arms around my neck and hugged me tightly. "I'm not going anywhere," she assured me. "I'm going to go shower," she let me know.

I laid in the bed and thought about what we were doing. The game we were playing was a dangerous one where there were two outcomes. We could either both be happy together or one of us was going to get hurt. With the way I felt about Happy, I couldn't afford to be the one who got hurt in this. Me hurting meant more than it did for her. I had to be everything and more for my mother and daughter. For five years, I had walked around broken from losing my first love. When I lost Tamia, I knew I would never find love like ours ever again. I didn't find love like Tamia and I had, it was different. What I had found was something that my heart, body, and soul had been lacking for five years. I continued to climb that ladder at work and accomplished all the goals I had set in place for my career. After I clocked out and came home to lay in my bed, I was still that guy from five years ago, in the same headspace.

I heard knocking and leaned my head up. "Baby, we're about to head upstairs," my mother said from the other side of the door.

Getting up, I went and opened the door. "I need to talk to you, mama."

"Everything all right?" A look of worry spread across her face.

"Everything is fine, Happy just needs to get away. I was thinking about staying in Dubai for a few extra days."

She took a sigh of relief. "Boy, don't start a conversation off with your facial expression and the words *I need to talk to you, mama,*" she laughed.

"Sorry."

"I think that's a good idea for the both of you. Colt, when I moved here, I moved here to make your life easier. You work hard and provide both me and River with a good life. We just want you to be happy, baby." She reached up and massaged my shoulder.

"I... I just feel bad about leaving and not spending enough time with River."

"River is fine. She knows that everything you're doing is for her. How can you be great for her if you don't take time to get your mental right? You haven't been happy since Tamia died. You've done a good job with masking your emotions and your unhappiness, however, I'm your mother and I knew you were hiding it. Me and River are fine. Go have a good time and both of you come back rested and ready to take on life."

I pulled my mother into a hug. "Ma, sometimes I feel like I don't deserve you."

She kissed me on the cheek. "Baby, the way I prayed for you, you can never lose when you have a praying mother. If your grandmother was alive, she would be proud of the man and father you have become. Get some sleep and tell Happy we said goodnight and we hope she has a better morning." She kissed me once more before she walked down the hall. I pulled my clothes off and went into the bathroom where Happy was standing under the showerhead, allowing the water to trickle down her entire body. Opening the glass shower door, I stepped in and tapped her. When she turned around, I realized she was crying under the water and using the sounds of the shower to muffle her sobs.

"Tell me what's wrong." I pulled her into my chest and she continued to cry into my chest. "Please, baby," I begged. I needed to know what was wrong with her. She was sobbing hard into my chest.

"I... I can't. I don't want you to look at me different," she stammered in between sobs. Pulling her closer, I wrapped my arms around her naked body and held her. We allowed the water to fall all over our bodies and stood there silently.

I wanted her to know that nothing she said to me could ever change how I felt about her. Whatever she was feeling right now was in the past. I was determined to be her future and she had to know that I cared about how she felt. I wasn't a man who was going to disregard her feelings. So many women often fought silent battles because their men weren't men. Instead of listening to them, giving them the strength they needed during their weakest moment, they allowed women to fight their battles alone. She didn't have to tell me right now or ever, but I was still going to be that rock to hold her when she needed it the most.

Dubai, UAE

Happy was sleeping peacefully in our room while I sat out on the balcony, looking at the beautiful cityscape Dubai had to offer. The flight was smooth sailing. Happy had managed to get a last-minute first class flight on the plane, which was good. When I was taking my break, I went up to her pod and checked in on her. Most of the time, she was asleep. We had just landed a few hours ago and she was sleeping again. Whatever was going on with her must have been deep. Everything about her seemed off and I just wanted to fix her. My mother always said I should have been a doctor.

Even as a child, she said I always wanted to fix people. I wasn't one to sit and watch someone hurt. If I could help it, I wanted to help them the best I could. Before we left to the airport, we headed to her house so she could pack some clothes and grab her passport. I asked if she wanted to turn her phone on and call her parents to let them know, and she refused. Even now, her phone was still off.

On the way to the hotel, I called my mother and told her that I landed. She did her usual prayer with me and told me to have a great few days. This wasn't like me. First Bora Bora, now Dubai. Since having River, I didn't do all the traveling I did like when I was younger. My life literally revolved around her, so I worked and came home. Being in Dubai and not having to work felt like everything to me. I had spoken with my boss about not flying back and taking on the flight that left in a few days. He was pissed for the late notice, but because I hadn't taken time off since I started, he agreed. Besides Bora Bora, all I did was work. By law, I was only allowed to fly a thousand hours a year. I usually took short flights, and rarely would I take on a long flight like this one. Because the end of the year was coming and I was almost to my max thousand hours, I decided it would be best to take some time off in between working.

"Why aren't you sleeping? Didn't you fly the last few hours here?" Happy yawned as she came out onto the balcony. She moved my legs and sat on my lap.

I reached up and removed her curly hair from her face. "You okay now?"

"I think so."

"You gonna tell me what happened, Happy?"

She kissed me on the lips and I broke our kiss. "What?" she questioned.

"Tell me."

She pulled her thick hair into a bun and stared out at the cityscape before she turned her attention back to me. "I really don't want to bring it up again."

"Happy, you need to tell me. If that shit got you breaking down the way you were, you need to tell me what's going on with you."

"I was raped when I was seventeen years old," she revealed. I could hear the shakiness of her voice when she spoke. "I called my sister and asked her for a ride, but her boyfriend answered. She was too drunk to drive, so he picked me up. Long story short, he raped me that night."

My fucking heart broke for her. I watched her facial expression as she told me and I could see the disgust on her face. She damn near choked out the words. I sighed because that shit was fucked up all around. No woman should ever have to be raped, and men who raped were fucking cowards in my book.

"Did he go to jail?"

"No, he went on to marry my older sister. I've had to hold this secret in for years. While everyone sees me as Happy and I'm smiling and living my life, I'm depressed and I've worked hard, trying to push and keep this in the past. At Thanksgiving dinner, he was there and everything came back and hit me in my gut, and I revealed it to my family.

"Wait, nobody in your family knew? Babe, you should have told someone."

"I told my mother and she told me to keep my mouth shut. She blamed me and told me that I shouldn't have been wearing that short dress. She claimed that if I dressed like a wholesome girl, I wouldn't have been mistaken for a slut."

My jaw became tensed and I looked at her. "You mean to tell me you came to your mother as a teenage girl who was raped and she blamed you and allowed your older sister to marry the rapist?"

"Yes."

If something like that happened to River, I would probably be sitting in prison, waiting for the needle to be put in my vein. Clothes didn't make men rape, men raped because of them. I was so tired of people blaming women, their clothes or action on the reason they were raped. It wasn't women who stuck their dick where it didn't belong, it was men.

"I'm so sorry." I pulled her close and hugged her tightly. "I'm so sorry that happened to you." I continued to whisper in her ear as she cried.

This woman had to hold this in while this man was welcomed around her family for years. Having to battle with rape was one thing, but having the rapist become a part of your family was another thing. Her mother not only allowed her oldest daughter to marry him, but she also told her youngest daughter to shut her mouth about what happened to her. That shit was fucked up and made me wonder what the hell else her mother had probably hidden from the family.

"I appreciate you and your family for welcoming me in. Being in your home, it feels so comfortable and natural being around you guys. Your mother is such a wonderful and caring woman. Then, your daughter, she has many reasons she could hate me and her face lights up whenever she sees me."

Touching her face, I stared right into her eyes. "I want us to be more, Happy. Since I've met you, I had a good feeling about you. It wasn't a coincidence that you happened to be late that morning to the airport and bumped right into me. Or, the fact that you were boarding my plane. Then, we were seated right next to each other and stayed at the same resort. Things like that don't happen by coincidence, that was fate."

"Colt, I love you. I've been battling with the feelings I've felt and trying to sort them out. I've prayed and questioned if it was nuts to fall in love with someone you just met. How could you get me and haven't known me more than a month or two? I feel more comfortable with your family than my own. How is that?" I didn't say anything. From her expression, I could tell the insecurity was settling. "I'm sorry. I told myself that it was too much." She back peddled.

I swooped her up and brought her back into the room. Tossing her onto the bed, I pulled her panties up and mounted her. Looking into her eyes as I pushed myself deeper and deeper inside of her, I replied, "I love you, Happy. I didn't fight with the feelings because I've been in love before and I know what it feels like. What we have is love, I can tell you that much."

She wrapped her legs around my waist and pushed her lips onto mine. "Make love to me, Colt," she moaned. I kissed her and did just as she requested. I always laughed at people who could fall in love in a matter of months, and here I was, a man who had met a woman and had been captivated with everything about her in a short amount of time. Everything about Happy made me happy. I wanted to spend the rest of my life making her happy.

Chapter Eleven

HI, SKELETONS... MEET THE CLOSET

Happy

"I so appreciate you picking and dropping me off. I forgot Mom and Dad were going to Savannah to have dinner with your parents," I thanked my sister's boyfriend.

It was prom night, and I had partied my night away with my friends. This was our senior year and we had definitely partied super hard. Everyone else had boyfriends who they were going to a hotel with, but me, I had myself and I was ready to go. My best friend, Anna, tried to convince me to go with her to her boyfriend's vacation house in North Carolina. I wasn't interested in being locked in a car with Anna and her drunk boyfriend. I called Jade and Tony answered the phone. The two of them didn't live together, but Tony was always at Jade's condo, more than his own. He had told me that Jade had a little too much to drink at dinner and that he didn't mind coming to pick me up. I was relieved that I didn't have to bum a ride from someone in my class.

Tony arrived in twenty minutes, put his sweater around my shoulders, then held the door open for me. He was such a gentleman and I was proud that he was my sister's boyfriend. It was nice to have a big brother figure.

My mother had all girls and she had miscarried our brother years back. After me, she stopped trying and decided to put her all into her girls. The Blatimore brothers were the brothers all the white girls at my school spoke about. Nine times out of ten, if they showed up home with a black man, their parents would shit their pants. However, if they showed up with a Blatimore brother, their parents knew their future was secured. Most of the girls I went to school with didn't have any goals of going to college. The plan was to find a rich husband and start their family immediately. Being that both my sisters were in a relationship with Tommi and Tony Blatimore, those girls in school had to find other suitable husbands.

"You know you're like a little sister to me. I'm sorry your sister got too smashed to come pick you up."

"It's fine. Why did she get drunk? Jade doesn't drink often." Jade was a lightweight when it came to alcohol. The only time she chose to indulge in a drink was when there was a celebration happening.

"We're engaged. It's the reason your parents decided to head down to Savannah. They're celebrating our engagement," he smiled.

"Wow! Congratulation, Tony. I know and see how much you love my big sister. I'm so happy for you guys!" I squealed.

"Thank you, sis," he said as he pulled into the driveway.

"Of course. I feel so bad asking you to pick me up on the night you got engaged. Come in, we'll pop a bottle of Mom's champagne and toast. We'll have one glass."

"Hap, you're like fifteen," he chuckled.

"Um, excuse you? I'm seventeen and I'll be eighteen in a few months." I was offended at him getting my age wrong.

"I know. I'm kidding." He laughed as he looked up from his phone. "On second thought, I'll come have that toast."

"Good." I climbed out of the car and tried my best to pull my dress down. I wore a gold silk dress that stopped just above my thigh with slits around the midsection. My body looked perfect in it. I worked out with a trainer the entire school year just to achieve this look tonight.

I let us into the house and realized my mother had given the staff the night off. Usually, when I came home, there was someone here. "Nobody home?"

"I guess not. Mama must have been feeling generous tonight," I giggled. "I'll grab the champagne from the wine cellar and we'll toast. I feel like I deserve a toast. I'm graduating high school and I'm graduating with a 4.0." I bragged on myself a bit.

"Well, we'll toast to that, too." He walked toward the kitchen with his hands shoved into his pockets.

I took my heels off and headed down the stairs to the wine cellar. My father loved wine. He built this cellar when I was a year old. My mother was more of a champagne lover and they combined his love for wine and her love for champagne and created a room down here. One room was the cellar for my father's wine, and the other room was my mother's champagne room. I turned on the light and pressed the security code on the door that protected the wine and champagne. My father had wines that were older than him and valued at half a million dollars. So, I understood why he kept it heavily secured down here.

I skimmed my mother's selection and settled on Armand de Brignac Brut Gold. As I turned around, I bumped right into Tony.

"Good Lord, you scared the hell out of me." I tried to steady my breathing.

"How you gonna use Lord and hell in the same sentence?" He laughed and took the bottle of champagne out of my hand. "This is what you chose? Cool. I can dig it." He walked over to the bar my mother had down in her room.

"We should head back upstairs. My parents hate when I'm down here."

"Are your parents here? And they're all the way in Savannah. Makes no sense to go back up there, we can pop it here and enjoy the bottle."

"That's true." I climbed up on the stool and watched as he popped the bottle. "I just love the smell of champagne."

"This is how I know we're privileged. Who else opens a bottle of six thousand dollar champagne?"

"Children of wealthy parents. But, you'll be running your father's company soon enough."

"I can't wait to travel the world and do what he does. For years, when he missed birthdays, holidays and important events, I always questioned

why. I'm older now and I see he was traveling the world, buying and selling real estate."

"You're going to make an amazing broker. With Jade and her wedding planning business, you both are going to be the power couple of Atlanta."

"I hope so."

"I know so."

"And you?"

"What about me?"

"What are you going to do soon as you graduate?"

"Daddy says I have to go to school for business first. He says I need to have a degree, but Mama couldn't care less. She wants me to marry rich," I joked, however, it was the truth.

"And what do you want?"

"I want to style people. I love fashion and I just want to do whatever allows me to do that and provide me with wealth. This dress, I designed it myself and worked with the seamstress myself."

"Oh, really?"

"Yes. My mom hated it, but I knew everyone would love it at prom tonight."

"Your boyfriend probably loved it the most."

"Yeah, if he was still my boyfriend. His stupid self showed up with the girl I saw him kissing at a party." I sighed. "I don't need a man to appreciate this dress. I appreciate it and that's all that matters." I accepted the glass of champagne from him.

"To us." He held up the glass and we clinked glasses. I took a sip of mine and placed it down. "So, about you and Jade. When's the wedding?"

"I'm gonna leave that to her. You know she loves and knows everything about weddings."

"True." Jade was an intern for a well-known wedding planner here in Atlanta. This was her passion and something she was serious about. She had plans of opening up her own business where she would plan weddings. Right now, she was gaining all the experience she could working as an intern.

"Why you staring at me like that?" Tony chuckled as he poured more champagne into his flute.

"Huh? I was just thinking to myself." I waved him off. "You should get back to Jade. I appreciate you having a talk with me."

He finished another glass of champagne and made his way around the bar. His aura changed and he was making me feel uncomfortable. His eyes looked as if he was undressing me with them. His hand trailed up my exposed thighs and I slapped them.

"Don't be like that, Happy."

"Stop, Tony. You're about to marry my sister. What do you mean, don't be like that?"

"Happy, you in that dress, wanting to have champagne with me... you wanted this." He grabbed a handful of his dick.

"Uhh, you're tripping." I laughed and jumped down from the stool. I turned my back to head upstairs and he grabbed me. "Get the hell off of me." I snatched my arm away from him.

"Happy, you know how bad your sister wanted this? Your mother made her wait and save her virginity just for me to take."

"I'm not Jade and I don't even look at you like that... Eww."

His facial expression changed. "What the hell you mean, eww?"

"You're not my damn type."

"I'm everybody's type."

"Well, not mine," I laughed. "You need to leave and I won't mention this to your future wife."

He grabbed me by the arm and pulled me closer to him. Wrapping his hand around my neck, he pushed me over to the plush couch and pulled at my dress. I couldn't scream because of the pressure he was applying to my neck. It was like a nightmare I was trying hard to wake up from and couldn't. He yanked my panties down and struggled with trying to get them off, so he pulled one time and ripped them off, causing fabric burn on my thigh. Tears welled up in my eyes and poured down the side of my face. Why was he doing this to me? I didn't ask for this and I damn sure didn't deserve this. He loosened his slacks and allowed them to drop to the floor. I felt him force himself inside of me several times before he was fully in.

I laid there as he continued to rape me. Eventually, his hand came from around my neck and I laid there. Instead of fighting, I laid there and sobbed as he finished up and pulled his pants up. He stared down at me with a crooked smirk fixed on his face as he fastened his belt. I laid there with my panties on the floor and my dress ripped from the bottom. If I had a gun, I wouldn't have shot him, but I would have shot myself in the head. In this moment, all I wanted to do was die. This man was around my family, he had known me since I was a baby, and he raped me.

"Oh, stop... you know you wanted it," he laughed. "Don't worry. It's our little secret... isn't that what you said?" He chuckled as he grabbed the bottle of champagne and guzzled it, then left me downstairs.

It took me an hour to collect myself from the couch. Everything down below hurt like hell. There was blood on my mother's suede sofa and my dress was soiled. In a state of shock, I cleaned up everything. My mother always told me you cleaned any stain with club soda, and that was what I did. I made sure to blot the stain out, straighten up the bar, rinse the glasses, then collect my torn panties and carry myself upstairs. I ran a bath and sat in the tub. I went under the water and held my breath, wanting to end it all. The phone in my bathroom rang and I came back up and tried to catch my breath. Reaching out the tub, I grabbed the cordless phone and pressed the button.

"Hello?" I whimpered.

"Happy? Girl, what the hell are you doing home on prom night, and why do you sound like your dog died?" Kharisma nearly yelled through the phone.

Wiping my face, I tried to fix my tone. "I'm in the tub. Prom wasn't all that."

"I'm sorry, pooh. Well, I was calling to let Daddy know that I passed finals," she squealed in excitement.

"Oh, really? Congrats, Khar. I'm happy for you."

"Well, you don't sound like it. What's going on, Happy? Do I need to come home?"

I counted to six and switched my tune. "Me and Anna got into it. She chose her boyfriend over me, but I'm cool. Tell me more about the finals."

"Finals are boring. I only wanted to ace because Mama was in Daddy's ear about me coming home because I was wasting time with college."

"Is she still on you about Tommi?"

"Ugh, you know it. She feels I need to come home and be a girlfriend."

"Well, you know Mama. Ton..." I choked.

"Huh?"

"Tony and Jade got engaged."

"I knew it was coming. All Jade talks about is being his wife. I bet she plans her entire wedding alone."

"No need to bet me, I already know it."

"Anyway. I'm about to head to the bar with some friends to celebrate. I'm sorry prom sucked, but there won't be too many events that will suck when you're a famous stylist. Love you, Happy, and I'll call tomorrow when the parents are home."

"Thanks, Kharisma. Talk to you soon," I replied and ended the call. After I ended the call, I sat in the tub for hours, thinking about everything that had just occurred. I truly felt broken inside.

"This gala is going to be one to remember. I need everything to go off without a hitch. The Galleria name is on it," my mother spoke to her team of interns and assistant, all who were helping her plan my father's charity gala he threw every year right before the new year.

Everyone who was everyone came to our annual Galleria Gala that gave back to women who suffered domestic violence. My grandmother went through domestic violence and had no one to turn to. It was a charity that was near and dear to my father's heart, so he put my mother in charge of picking a theme and making sure everything was perfect. This year's theme was Great Gatsby. My mother didn't work, and now that both my sisters were out the house and I was soon on my way out, she needed something to do. My father put her in charge of handling all the charity's business.

"Mama, can I speak to you?"

My mother stopped talking and turned her attention to me. "One sec, baby doll. Let me wrap this up and we can chat." She smiled at me. My mother was a beautiful woman. Her smile could light up a room. It was one of the things my father said I inherited from her.

I sat outside my dad's study, shaking my right leg out of nervousness. I was so nervous to tell my mother what happened two days ago. For two days, I tossed and turned, couldn't eat or focus in class. With school coming to an end, I needed to focus on my exit exams. Still, the look that came across Tony's face was a constant memory when I closed my eyes. I dreamed of the day I would fall in love and give my boyfriend, fiancé, or even husband the gift of taking my virginity. While my friends in school were all having sex, I was saving myself. Everyone always questioned if I was saving myself for marriage and that wasn't the case. I was saving myself for love. I wanted to be so madly in love with whoever I chose to give my virginity to.

With what Tony did to me, I felt soiled, dirty and no longer worthy of anyone's love. How could someone love me? A girl who was raped by her sister's fiancé. My friend Anna tried to get what was wrong out of me and I screamed at her. I didn't mean to scream at her and say hurtful words to her and I regretted some of the words that came out of my mouth.

"Baby child, why are you out here shaking like that?" My mother deterred me from my thoughts.

"Mama, I really need to talk to you... alone."

"I have to head downtown to your father's office, so come up to my room and tell me while I change," she replied, taking my hand.

We headed up to her and my father's suite and I sat down on her ottoman while she pulled an equally fabulous outfit out and laid it on her bed. My mother was such a pageant queen. While she had never won one pageant, she carried herself like she was Ms. America herself.

"Happy, you wanted to talk?" she reminded me.

"Mom, something happened the night of prom," I started. She picked out the matching accessories to her outfit while she listened.

"Uh-huh... prom. What happened at prom?"

"I didn't want to stay anymore, so I called Jade to pick me up. Tony said she had too much to drink and she couldn't drive, so he offered to pick me up," I paused.

"Aw, that was sweet of him. He's going to make a good husband," she muttered.

"He drove me home and told me that he and Jade got engaged."

"Oh, Happy, this wedding is going to be beautiful. Your sister is already getting her magazines ready to plan the wedding of the century." She raved about Jade's wedding.

"We decided to toast with a bottle of your champagne. You know, since he was engaged and I'm about to graduate at the top of my class."

"Baby, you know me and Daddy are both so proud of how you have excelled in school."

"Thanks, mom."

"And you were saying?" she asked.

"Tony raped me, mama." I broke down. "He pulled at my panties and raped me." My mom looked at me horrified. "He pulled at my panties and forced himself into me. Mom, he took my virginity."

My mother sat down next to me and rubbed my shoulders. "Baby, are you sure you didn't make the mistake of sleeping with your sister's fiancé?"

I stared up at my mother. "Mom, I know what sex is and I know what rape is and he raped me."

She stood up and sat at her vanity. I stared at her through the mirror as she stared back at me. She took her earrings off and replaced them with ones that were suitable for her outfit.

"Happy Joy Galleria, who else have you said this to?"

"Just you."

"Good."

"Mama, it hurt so bad. I want him to go to jail." I cried to her.

She applied her infamous red lipstick across her lips. "Happy, we will not get the authorities involved in this. I tell you one thing... I was right."

"Right about what, mama?"

"That damn dress. I told you that dress was going to attract the wrong attention, and look, it did."

"Mama, my dress didn't rape me, Tony did," I cried.

"Enough, Happy. Do you know what your sister is about to marry into? The Blatimore family is wealthier than us. You put that out there that their oldest son is a rapist and our family will be blackballed. Your father has worked very hard on everything we have. Do you really want to see his hard work go down the drain? Moving forward, you won't wear that type of clothing any longer. And, we'll get you into therapy. Don't speak a word of this to your father," she spoke through the mirror.

"But, ma—"

"You heard me. Now, excuse me, I need to go down to the cellar and deal with something." She got up from her vanity and left the room.

I sat there with tears streaming down my eyes, hurt. My mother had basically blamed me for what happened to me. Because of Tony's last name, I couldn't speak about what happened to me. It was a secret both me and my mother had to take to the grave – together.

Chapter Twelve

TOO GOOD AT GOODBYES

Happy

Dubai was everything and more. It was a nice getaway from all the drama that was currently surrounding my life. After I told Colt I loved him, I expected him to distance himself from me. It was the complete opposite and it made my heart smile. While in Dubai, we did everything, took pictures, and made love until the sun came up. It sounded crazy that I was in another country, living my best life with a man other than my boyfriend. Phil and I didn't travel or do fun things because he was always so consumed with work. For once, I wanted him to tell me that he had taken off from work and wanted to spend time with me. It was wishful thinking because Phil would never take off from work, even if it was an emergency with his own family.

It was different when it came to Colt. He hadn't even known me long and had taken off from work just so I could get away. The way he was so attentive to my needs made me feel like this was a cruel joke. God wouldn't send me someone so perfect like him without consequences to follow. Colt made me feel like a real woman who could do anything she put her mind to. When he found out about me being raped, I expected him to judge me. Instead, he cradled me, told me how much I meant to him and made me feel like a woman. The way he spoke to me made my stomach fill with butterflies. When he cocked his head to the side and smirked at me, I just wanted to melt into a pool of water.

We had been back from Dubai for three days and I had yet to turn my phone on. Instead of going home, I had been hiding out at Colt's house. His home felt comfortable to me. It was as if I had known his mother and daughter my entire life. Like now, he was off to work and I was sitting on his bed, listening to his mother cough and get River ready for school. I pulled Colt's Brooklyn Nets hoodie over my head and went into the kitchen. Colt's mother, Nia, was sitting on the couch with a napkin in her hand, coughing while trying to get River ready for school.

"Mama Nia, you need to go back to bed. I can hear you coughing from the bedroom," I advised as I sat down next to her.

"After my doctor told me I had the flu, you would think I would," she laughed, then broke out into a coughing fit. Colt is off to work and I need to get River to school."

"I'm here. I can take her to school."

"Oh, baby, you're relaxing. I'm fine."

"No, I'm fine. I've been in the house for three days and I need to get out. I can take your car and grab some groceries to make some chicken soup... I make a good chicken soup."

She was hesitant but agreed. "Okay, please be safe. Colt is coming back tonight, too, so I'll get up to clean later." I loved that even while she was sick, she was still adamant about taking care of their home.

"Let's just see how you're feeling later. Now, up to bed." I pulled her up and walked her over to the stairs. "I promise I'll get her to school."

"Granny, you need to rest. Miss Happy will get me to school." River hugged her grandmother.

"When I prayed for a good woman to come into Colt's life, I

didn't remember mentioning I wanted her to be as pushy as me." She let out a chuckle.

"Well, God gives us exactly what we need. Off to bed."

"All right, all right... I'm going. Riv, have a great day at school."

"Thank you, Granny," she replied.

I grabbed the car keys, my purse, and Brownie and headed out the door with River. River held Brownie as I pulled out the driveway and headed out the subdivision. River bopped her head to music while I was deep in thought. Colt had left last night on a redeye to Mexico. He stayed overnight and was due to be back tonight. Even with him being gone for a day, I missed him like crazy.

"Do you love my daddy?" River broke our silence and pulled me from my thoughts. I smiled as I made a right like the GPS suggested.

"I do. Why do you ask?"

"He deserves the kind of love in the movies."

"Naw, that love is fake. Your daddy deserves real love."

"I agree," she giggled. "Are you going to give him babies, and are you gonna get married? Granny was talking to her friend about it."

I blushed because I hadn't thought that far. "Right now, we're taking it slow. I'm not saying that it won't happen, just not right now."

"Okay."

It was so funny that not once did I think of getting married or having Colt's babies. With Phil, I thought about those things constantly. I guess it was because his presence was lacking in our relationship, so I wanted something to occupy my time. Maybe I wanted something where he would show me just a quarter of attention. Marriage and babies were what came to mind when I thought about Phil. After spending so much time with Colt, I realized I didn't want to be married to a man like Phil. A man who was so married to his work that I came last. It wasn't a good feeling when your boyfriend chose to stay late at the office instead of coming over to your house to spend time with you. Our sex life was nonexistent. With him working more and too occupied to spend time with me, we had quickies. I couldn't remember the last time we had made love. Even then, the way he made love and the way Colt made love were two different experiences.

We pulled up at the car pool line and I unlocked the doors and took Brownie from River. "Have a great day, hun," I told her.

"Thanks, Miss Happy. You too." She smiled before she hopped out and ran into the school. I sat Brownie down on the seat and he jumped to try and look for River. Since he had been with River, he had grown quite attached to her.

"Sorry, buddy, we'll see her later." I put Publix's address into the GPS and headed there.

I sat in the driveway with all the grocery bags. My phone was in my hand and I flipped it around like it was a foreign object. My phone had been off since Thanksgiving, and here it was, about to be December in two days. I pressed the top button and powered on my phone. The apple popped up on the screen. While the phone powered up, I looked over at a sleeping Brownie in the passenger seat. As soon as the password screen popped up, a bunch of text messages and missed calls appeared on my screen. I had a bunch of emails, Instagram DMs and message board messages from my blog. Just when I was about to grab Brownie, then grab the rest of the bags, my phone started to ring. It took just a second for the name to register. Kharisma's name popped up, followed by a few emojis. I slid my finger across the screen and answered.

"Hey," I whispered. Kharisma was the loudest of all three of us, so I knew she was going to chew into my ass about going ghost for an entire week.

"Hey? Happy Joy Galleria, do you know how many times I've called you? Dad called me and told me what happened and said you weren't home or answering your phone. But, you bought a plane ticket to Dubai." I sucked my teeth because I knew using the debit card attached to my trust fund was a stupid idea. The money I needed for that flight wasn't in my regular accounts, so I had to tap into my funds.

"I just really needed to get away, Kharisma." I sighed into the phone. "I should have called and let you know what was going on, but I didn't and I apologize for that."

Her tone softened. "I heard what Tony did and it explains why you've had all this hate for him all these years. I'm sorry, Happy. Is that why you sounded that way when I called that night?"

"Yes."

"I should have known. I should have flown home and been there with you."

"It's not your fault so don't blame yourself," I told her.

"As your sister, I should have noticed something was off with you. You pulled back from a lot of stuff and refused to be in Jade's wedding. That was a huge sign and I didn't see it."

"Khar, it wasn't your place to protect me. It happened and it's over."

"Can you believe Jade left for Singapore with that bastard?" she informed me of my sister's recent actions.

"No, I didn't know."

"Yes, she didn't say much about the incident and still went to Singapore with that asshole."

"I can't say I'm surprised. Khar, I appreciate you checking on me, but I'm safe."

"Where are you?"

"Lawrenceville."

"Lawrenceville? What's in Lawrenceville?"

"Colt."

She gasped. "Colt, the pilot? You guys are doing it like that?"

"We said I love you. He was with me in Dubai."

"You paid for his flight, Happy?"

I was pissed she would ask that. "He was the one flying the plane. Khar, I'm gonna say this once and that's it. Colt doesn't want me for my money and doesn't give a damn what my last name is. If anything, he was the one who paid for the entire Dubai trip."

"Okay, I'm sorry. You know I just want to make sure you're not being taken advantage of. Ten thousand dollars for a flight was a lot of money."

"I wish everyone would stay out my account. I've never made a big purchase since I've been given access to it. If I want to blow money on a flight, then that's my business."

"Happy, you're being snippy with the wrong one. I'm just trying to see if you're okay and ask questions that everyone is wondering. How can I be on your side if I know nothing?"

"Sorry. Your comment about him using me for money pissed me off."

"And I apologize about that. Now, what is going on with Phil?"

"I'm breaking up with him."

"You're what?"

"Breaking up with him," I repeated in case she hadn't heard me the first time.

After spending time with Colt in Dubai, I took a day to myself and went to the spa. I sat in the spa sauna, thinking about what my next steps would be. First, I knew I would have to confront my family, then I knew I would have to deal with Phil. For so long, I blocked out the fact that I was unhappy with Phil. I tried to convince myself that it would get better or that we needed a commitment, even a baby. Being around Colt, and seeing how he made me feel so alive made me realize that I needed to end things with Phil. Phil was married to his job and that was fine. He couldn't have me any longer and there was a reason why I hadn't moved anything into his condo since he had given me the key. God gave you signs and sometimes you didn't even realize the signs He was giving you were blessings in disguise.

"Earth to Happy," Kharisma's voice blared through the phone.

"Sorry."

"While I'm happy that you're breaking up with him because you deserve better, I just want you to make sure it's the right choice for you."

"I know it's the right choice. I've never been so sure of something in my life. There's not much to end. We haven't been a couple in a long time. It's been him and his job, and I was the physical aspect when he needed a date for important events."

"And what's going to happen with Colt?"

"What do you mean?" I questioned as I struggled through the door with Brownie and the bags.

"Are you guys going to be together?"

"We haven't got that far yet."

"Hap, I just need to lay eyes on you. Can I come to you?"

"Sure. What time you get off?"

"I'm off. I can come over now," she offered. "Just text me the address."

"I'll send it to you," I replied and we ended the call.

Ms. Nia came down the stairs when she heard me in the kitchen. "I got as much rest as I'm going to get," she tried to convince me.

"Ms. Nia, I was barely gone two hours. That's not enough rest."

"For a busy body like me, it is. I won't do nothing, but let me sit in here and talk to you. It's nice to have someone here when River and Colt are both gone."

"It's nice to have someone to talk to other than myself."

"I feel like a crazy lady sometimes when I talk to myself. What kind of chicken soup you about to make?"

I smiled. "My nanny used to make it for me when I was sick. She added chicken, turkey tail and a bunch of seasoning in it with egg noodles."

"Turkey tails?"

"It's weird, but it's delicious. Trust me."

"Okay, I'm gonna trust you." She was hesitant.

"My sister wants to stop by and see me. I told her it was fine, I hope you don't mind."

She waved me off. "I don't mind. The more the merrier."

"You're a good woman, Ms. Nia."

"Baby, I try," she smiled. "Now, tell me what happened with you," she questioned. Ms. Nia made me feel so comfortable. I explained what happened to me and she gasped while holding her mouth. "And your mama knew? Jesus Christ."

"Yes, I forgave my mother years ago." I had my back turned as I washed my hands and felt a hug from behind.

I was around 5'5, and Ms. Nia was shorter than me. She had to be around five feet even. I turned around and hugged her tightly. "Thank you."

"My door is always open to you. Always," she replied. "Now, get to cooking." She laughed and I got to chopping up onions.

I sat on the couch with Ms. Nia and chatted about *Love & Hip Hop: New York*. We were enjoying the drama on the show while eating our bowls of soup. Kharisma had called me and told me that she had a patient being rushed to the hospital and she had to head there. We made plans to catch brunch at a café near Colt's house and ended the call. Ms. Nia never did go upstairs, but she didn't clean either. I cooked, cleaned, and made sure River did her homework. Before she went to bed, we read some articles off TMZ. According to Ms. Nia, it was River's favorite thing to do.

Colt said his flight got delayed and he wouldn't get home until tomorrow, so sitting on the couch and chatting with his mom was the next best thing to do. We spent all day together and I still wasn't tired of this lady. I soaked in all her wisdom because she had a lot of it. When I complained about my career, she gave me something to think about. She told me that I had the gift and resources to make something out of myself and not many had those blessings. I could style a pig and make women envious of a pig and my father owned one of the top department stores in Atlanta. He had done campaigns with so many celebrities, and I was sure he had their contacts but I had never asked my dad. I always assumed he wouldn't help me because I had quit working for him.

The front door jingled and Ms. Nia and I looked at each other. "You heard that?"

"Yes. I have my phone, run to the bathroom just in case." I

stood up and walked to the foyer.

"Happy, you were raised in a rich home. We stick together. I'm rocking and you rolling," she said as we crept to the front.

"Why the hell y'all creeping like that?" We heard a voice and both jumped. When we turned around, Colt was coming out the closet downstairs.

"Baby!!" I ran into his arms and kissed him. He picked me up and swallowed me with his muscular arms. I had never missed someone like I missed Colt. It was weird, yet it felt nice, too.

"Dang, I get love like this?" he smiled. "Hey, mama."

"Boy, don't be coming up in here like that... me and Happy were gonna lay you out." She did Kung Fu movements.

"All right, Chun Li," he laughed. "Mama, you all right?" He heard the cold in her chest.

"Just the flu. Ms. Happy here wouldn't allow me to do anything and she made me this soup that's very good."

"Oh, yeah? I appreciate that."

"Of course. Your mom kept me company, I love her."

"Love you, too, Sweetie. I'm gonna take me my bowl upstairs and watch *Matlock*." She came over and kissed us both on the cheek before going to grab her bowl and going upstairs.

Colt carried me to the bedroom and placed me down on the bed. "Besides my mother and daughter, I ain't never had a reason to miss someone. You... you had me looking at our pictures in Dubai, counting down the hours until I could head back home."

I blushed because when he said it, I believed him. The way he stared into my eyes when he spoke let me know he was serious. "I missed you, too. You see I cleaned and washed your blankets."

"Oh, shit. Ms. Happy doing laundry."

"See, I didn't go that far," I smiled. "Take a shower and let me make you some soup. And we can watch this movie I found on Hulu."

"What movie? 'Cause that movie you picked in Dubai was weird."

"It's called *Downsizing*. I saw the trailer, it's not weird."

"Okay. I'm gonna go shower."

While he was in the shower, I went into the kitchen and heated up the soup. Grabbing a tray out the pantry, I put some crackers, soup and a bottle of Gatorade onto the tray and went to the bedroom. Colt finished in the shower soon after and we climbed into the bed.

"Did I tell you that I dropped River off to school today?"

"Yeah?"

"Uh-huh. Your mom was sick, so I went to drop her to school and grabbed some groceries." Something in his face changed. "What's wrong?"

"What are you gonna do with your situation? Hap, as much as I want you to stay here forever, you can't and have to face your family and boyfriend. I don't want my mother and daughter getting attached and then you leave. We got feelings, too, feel me?"

I completely understood what he meant. Colt made me feel alive and his family just added to that. Everything about him and his family made me excited for the future. Yet, I understood his fear. Anybody would have that same fear. Everything felt nice right now, but he knew it could change in a minute.

"I'm ending things with him. Colt, these past few days let me know that I *need* you. It's one thing to want someone, but to need them is different. I know we haven't been around each other long, and we have a bunch of stuff to learn about one another, but I'm excited to do that. I'm excited to see you mad and learn what makes you tick, and I'm excited for you to witness me act like a complete baby during my period. All these things don't sound appealing, still, it makes me excited for the journey."

"You really that bad on your period?"

"The worst," I admitted.

"I guess I better get chocolate... That's what y'all eat, right?"

"Uh-huh. And I get hungry every other hour. I think I gain around six pounds just during that five days."

He winked. "I like the extra meat, don't worry."

"Good to know. You ready to watch the movie?"

"Yeah, soon as I finish eating this good soup. You need to cook me something tomorrow."

"I don't mind."

"Babe, you been hiding, but you need to get back to work. Grab my laptop and sign into your emails and return people's messages. You wanted this and I'm not gonna let you sit here and not continue to chase your dreams."

"It's so fun not adulting."

"Yeah, that may be true, but you still need to build up your clientele, and sitting in my bedroom isn't going to do it."

"Fine," I pouted and grabbed the remote to start the movie. "I'll get to it tomorrow."

"I'm off this week, so I'm gonna make sure you do."

"Well, I need to go home and grab some more clothes, so can I take your car? I know you'll be asleep in the morning."

"Keys on the hook in the kitchen."

"Or should I take an Uber and drive my car back?"

"Whatever you want to do, babe," he replied and finished his soup.

We cuddled in bed and watched the movie. While spending this time with Colt, my mind couldn't help but think about Phil. The first couple of days he sent me a text message a day, then they stopped. Since I had turned my phone on, I hadn't heard anything from him. Not a call, text or email. It really showed me just how much I meant to him. His girlfriend, me, disappeared and you couldn't reach her, and you weren't calling her phone every hour on the hour? It was another slap in the face to let me know that his feelings weren't the same as mine. While I would be turning over every rock in Atlanta looking for him, he wasn't doing the same for me.

Colt had fallen asleep midway through the movie. Looking up at him, I smiled as I looked into his face. He was literally so perfect. I cuddled closer and closed my eyes and got some sleep. Like he said, I needed to get back to work and couldn't afford to slack because of my emotions.

Chapter Thirteen

IS THIS REAL? PINCH ME, GOD

Colt

I woke up to the sun shining in my face. Grabbing the cover, I pulled it over my face and tried to get more sleep. My body told me to stay in bed but my head wouldn't allow me to sleep for another second longer. Pulling the covers off me, I handled my morning hygiene and then went into the kitchen. My mother was sitting at the table with breakfast and tea. Happy let me know she was heading home to get more clothes and to grab her laptop. It was nice sharing my bed with someone. Not to mention, she helped with my mother and River. It took a lot of the stress off my mother and allowed her to get the rest she never wanted to take. I would be lying if I didn't admit I was scared. Scared of what? That she could change her mind and decide all of this was too much for her. Maybe one day she would wake up and decide she didn't want to take on a broken man, his daughter, and his aging mother. These were all things that came across my mind when I made love to her or held her in my arms at night.

"Hey, Ma!" I went to the coffee machine and brewed some coffee.

"Hey, baby boy. Happy is cooking tonight," she told me.

"She told you this?"

"Uh-huh. Said I'm not doing anything until the doctor clears me. Even said she'd go to the doctor with me."

"She committed to getting you back healthy."

"I really like her, son."

"I know you do. I love her."

"You told her that?"

"Yeah. She told me first."

"And what about this boyfriend? Is she willing to end things with him?"

"That's what she told me. She told me that she was going to end things with him and wanted to be with me."

My mama smiled widely. "I'm happy you found someone to make you happy. And the child's name is Happy." I laughed and checked the message that came across my phone.

Does your daughter go to Applewood elementary?

Azmina's name popped across the screen.

Why?

I'm substituting and I'm teaching a girl name River Wright. I remembered you had a daughter.

Lol yeah she goes there.

Oh wow small word. I'll tell her that me and you know each other.

Don't do that pls.

Um why?

I don't get my daughter involved in my personal life. That's all

Understandable.

Thanks.

Can we do dinner this week?

Can't.

K.

I didn't know how much more I had to tell Azmina that I wasn't interested anymore. The woman I wanted, I had. Azmina was cool and she would make an excellent wife to another man, that man just wasn't me. When she texted me, I was always busy and couldn't make time. I thought by making myself unavailable, she would catch the hint and leave me be. Instead, she always questioned when I was available and when we could hang out again. Happy and I had a lot to talk about when it came to starting a relationship. We weren't technically in a relationship, but we both made it clear that we wouldn't date anyone. She mentioned that Phil didn't count because he had to know their relationship was strained. All I wanted her to do was figure out the words she wanted to say and end it with him.

It slipped. Srry. & you have a gf? Wow.

I slapped my hand on my face and placed my phone on the table.

"Colt, why the hell you slapping yourself around?"

"Nothing, mama," I replied and grabbed my phone.

How does that slip? It's complicated.

Wow. You could have told me, jerk.

Just don't mention anything else to my daughter.

She never responded. I prayed that was the last time I had to hear from her. Now, I had to be questioned by River about me knowing her teacher. Azmina crossed the line by bringing my daughter into this. It wasn't her place to tell my daughter that we knew each other, especially after I had told her not to. What did she think we were going to do? Have an ice cream party and chat about how we had sex and I never saw her again? At the end of the day, the situation between us happened and she needed to move on like I had. When I thought back to that night, I wished I had never allowed things to go that far.

When she invited me in, I should have told her no and to have a good night. Except, I was pissed that Happy had basically dismissed me again for that fool, Phil. Two people were allowed to have sex and it not mean anything other than sex. Azmina needed to realize that what we had was sex and nothing more.

"Boy, you look like you're about to blow a gasket." My mother brought me from my thoughts.

"I'm good, mama."

"Don't look good."

"This girl I went on a date with is a substitute at River's school today."

"That's nice."

"Yeah."

She stared at me. "Did you sleep with this girl?"

"Something like that."

"It's either you did or you didn't, baby." She stood up and went to pour her some more tea.

"We did. I never said I wanted to be with her and we never said sleeping together was going to secure a spot in each other's lives."

"Some women don't think like that, Colt. Did you guys ever sit down and talk about what happened after you both decided to sleep together?"

"No." I was confused on why I needed to sit down and talk to her about us sleeping together. As humans, we picked up on vibes. I could tell if a woman wasn't interested in me and that told me how I should proceed. All the signals I sent to Azmina should have been enough for her to know that I was no longer interested. It wasn't like I went on the date looking forward to sleeping with her. She decided to set that mood, and as a grown man with needs, I went along with it, thinking we were two consenting adults just having fun.

"Well, I think you need to explain to her that you're not interested in being in a relationship with her. Something small like that will do wonders for a woman. It will let her know that the door to pursuing anything with you is closed."

"I hear you, Ma. I'm gonna go chill with Darrius." I kissed her on the cheek and went to shower and head over to his house. Kelli had had their son and I hadn't been over to see the baby because I had been occupied with my family, Happy and working. Darrius was on paternity leave and was driving himself crazy being home, so I wanted to go chill with him for a few hours until I had to pick River up from school.

When I arrived at Darrius's house, he was laying on the couch with his new son on his chest. Kelli was in the kitchen, pumping breastmilk, and the house was a mess. Bottles, clothes and baby accessories were spewed all around the house. Their house once felt like it was big enough for them, however with a new baby, you could tell they needed to consider moving into something bigger. Kelli yelled through their security ring bell that the door was open, so I was able to let myself in.

"Hey, Colt, how are you?" Kelli called from the kitchen.

"I'm good... how you feel?" I walked over and gave her a hug and kiss on the cheek. Even with two pumps hooked up to her breasts, she was chopping up onions and peppers for dinner.

"I'm good. Tired and trying to feel like myself again."

"You'll get there. You know if you need a babysitter, I'm here."

She cut her eyes at me. "I'm gonna hold you to that, too."

"For sure... hold me to it."

"Okay, Colt." She smiled and I went into the living room. Darrius was laying the baby down when I walked into the living room.

He put his finger over his mouth for me to be quiet and follow him into his garage, where his man cave was. Once he shut the door, he blew a sigh of relief. "Four more weeks of this paternity leave."

"You acting like it's a bad thing. You spending time with your family, man." I plopped down on the couch and kicked my feet up on the car tire coffee table.

"Man, Milani was so damn easy. Miles is something else. That boy can scream for hours and not take a break. Then Kelli been on my ass more than ever to find a new house."

"In her defense, you seen your crib? The baby is clearly here and is showing that he needs room."

He lit up a cigarette and leaned back in his recliner. "We can share Milani room."

"Why are you so hell-bent on not moving to something bigger?" I understood something big meant more money and he was probably scared about spending more money after just having a new baby. Still, they both needed to compromise on something because their house was closing in on them, and it was sure to start marital issues.

"Moving equals more bills. Bills equal me working more. Me working more equals Kelli complaining about I'm never home. And then the cycle repeats. She wants something bigger, not realizing that we have only one income: mine. We both come from the hood and we're used to sharing a room with two siblings at a time."

"You know they have houses for sale in my area. Not too expensive, safe and enough room for you all to grow. River would love being able to go to the same school as Milani."

"I'm not moving. We're good with this rental and Kelli better get used to it." He finished his cigarette and put it out in the ashtray. "So, with me having more time off from work, guess what I'm thinking of doing?"

"What?"

"Going on a mini vacation. Nowhere far, just to Vegas for the weekend. You down?" It was clear the settling life wasn't for Darrius. I didn't doubt he loved his daughter, but everything that came with being a parent, husband and responsible adult, he fought.

"Kelli going?"

"Nah. She's going to her mother's house in Florida for a week."

"Shouldn't you be going?"

"She don't want me to go. Milani has some more off time from school, so they're driving down there."

"Man, you really should go and be with your family."

He laughed. "Colt, she told me she didn't want me to go. Told me she needed time to think away from me."

"It's gotten that bad? The baby is only two weeks old."

"Hell yeah. We argue all the time and I go and get diapers and take hours because I need a break. Shit isn't peaches and cream like when we had Milani."

"Dang, I'm sorry to hear that. Maybe you both need to go to Vegas and let me take the kids. Me and Mama don't mind, and you know Mama know how to take care a baby."

He sat and debated before a smile spread across his face. "I do miss just spending time with my wife. These days, she got a baby stuck on her titty and then Milani trailing behind her with some assignment she need signed. It hasn't been just us in a long time and I think we both need time to reconnect."

"I mean, don't come back with another baby, but you get my point."

"Oh, I'm definitely hitting that before the six weeks," he smirked.

"Do you, man. Your wife means the world to you, and just because stuff isn't going as planned now doesn't mean you give up. She could tell you she hates you and doesn't want you to come to Florida, but deep inside, she's screaming for you to show her that you love her and want her here. Women are complex, yet simple creatures at the same time. You need to find your woman's language and you'll be straight for life."

"I appreciate you, man. You didn't come in here judging like my older brother did. Told me I was a stupid fool and I was going to lose the best thing I've ever did."

"He's right, too, but we as men have feelings, too. It isn't always about the woman. Yeah, they get the most attention because they give up their last name, have the babies, hold down the fort and remain fine as hell while doing it. Men battle depression and feel insecure, too. I think they're so used to us being macho that they forget we battle our own demons, too."

This man started jumping up and clapping his hands. "Preach, Brother Colt. Go on and preach my brother."

"Man, shut up." I laughed and took some peanuts out the can

on his coffee table. "I'm here to help. You know I'm always rooting for love."

"Yeah, speaking of love."

"Huh?"

"Catherine told me about your little Dubai trip." He spoke of one of the flight attendants who worked the flight when Happy and I went to Dubai.

"She got a big mouth. Cat need to worry about why her husband still hasn't moved to America." The woman had been dating a prince who lived in Africa. She believed it while all of us called her stupid behind her back. Clearly, he was one of those African men who poached women on social media for a ticket to America. Either way, you couldn't tell her that he wasn't a prince and it wasn't going to be much longer that she wouldn't be working this job.

"She do got a big mouth. Still, she told me that she saw you and your little friend kissing on the plane."

"Maybe."

"Maybe what? Y'all together or what?"

"Nah. We just vibing right now. I don't want to put a title on what we have until she ends things with her boyfriend."

"You slept with her?"

"Do I go around and ask you if you slept with Kelli? I'm a grown-ass man, Darrius. Not gonna sit here and talk about if I fucked."

"You're never any fun... So, where are the both of you at with this vibe?"

"She stays at the crib with me from time to time."

"Man, I could tell from that smile you're trying to hide that it's more than you putting on."

"I don't wanna speak prematurely. Ask me in another month."

"Fine, fine... How did that Tinder date go? I forgot to ask you," he mentioned. I filled him in on what happened and he was at the end of his seat, all wrapped into the story.

"You're the reason I'm in this mess."

"Me? How? I suggested going on a date, not busting the woman's back out where she stalking your child."

"She not stalking her... she working there today."

"Yeah... right. You both had sex as adults. There's no rule that says you have to be with her. Ms. Nia is right tho'. You need to sit down and talk to her about what happened and explain that you're not looking for a relationship from her."

"Yeah, I'll think about it.

"Call if you don't want to meet in person. You don't have to sit down and have coffee with her or nothing like that."

"Okay, I'll give her a call tonight."

"About Christmas."

"Uh-huh?"

"You remember the plan, right?"

"Dang, the cabin up in the mountains... forgot we planned that."

" I knew your ass did. Kelli and your mama been making sure we have everything. Is Happy invited?" He raised his eyebrow and stared at me.

"Don't know."

"Stop playing with me, Colt. You know I wanna know everything."

"In due time, my brother."

Happy had some things that needed to be sorted out before we put a label on what we had. While others felt like we were rushing into something, I had never felt so sure about something in my entire life. Everything about Happy let me know that I wanted this woman to be mine. When I say mine, I didn't mean just to have a girlfriend — I wanted to make her my wife in the future and I wanted her to have my babies. Happy had no idea what I wanted for her and our future. Her name was what I wanted her to always be when she woke up next to me.

Happy sat on the bed with her phone to her ear, talking to a client she had to meet tomorrow morning. The woman was going to a birthday dinner and needed her to style her for the dinner. Since she had turned her phone on, all she received was emails with people wanting to work with her. This was what she wanted and I was so happy to see her in her element. Closing the bedroom door, I went into the kitchen where my mother was stirring the gumbo she had made for dinner. We were born and raised in New York and knew nothing about gumbo, nonetheless, that didn't stop my mother from finding a recipe and attempting to make it.

"Dad, want to sit out back with me while Brownie poops?" River came over to me with her sweater in her hand.

"Of course."

We sat in the back on the patio and watched Brownie run around and play in the grass. River had never asked me for a dog so that was why we didn't have one. Seeing how happy and how responsible she was with Brownie made me smile. Happy had told her that she could have Brownie because she knew she could take care of him better than she could at the moment. My mother and I didn't have to give her a long speech about being responsible because she was already doing it. When she got up in the morning, she took him to use the bathroom, fed him, then was off to get herself prepared for the morning. It showed me just how much my daughter was growing up and how much she wasn't my baby anymore.

"Dad, my substitute teacher said she knew you the other day," River brought up. When I picked her up the other day, I decided not to mention the situation. If she didn't bring it up, it made no sense to bring light to the situation.

"Oh, you met my friend." I never lied to my daughter.

"How do you know her? Is she your type of friend like Ms. Happy?"

"No, babe. She's a friend I went on a date with. That's all. Ms. Happy is a special type of friend to me."

"Good. I like Ms. Happy. Will she be your wife in the future?"

"I sure hope so."

River smiled at me. "Mommy is smiling down on us. She knows that you deserve someone to love you like you love us."

"You guys love me, right?"

"Of course."

"Then I'm good."

"Not like me and Granny type of love. Like a love, love," she winked.

"Little girl, what you know about love, love?"

"I watch movies," she giggled. "Brownie, no!" she shouted to let him know to leave the tree branch alone.

"He listens to you."

"He does. I'm training him. He gets sad because Granny only allows him to sleep in a crate downstairs."

"Your room is always a mess, so you need to clean it so he can come up."

"He's fine downstairs," she cut me off.

I pushed her slightly. "You wanna keep him downstairs because you don't want to clean your room," I laughed.

"Noooo, I didn't say that."

"Yeah, right. Come on, let's head in, it's getting cold."

As soon as we came in, my mother was standing there with her hand on her hip. "When were you going to tell me that Kelli and Darrius were going to Vegas and we're watching Milani and Miles?"

"Dang, I forgot to mention it, mama."

"I'm glad you're feeling real friendly. Me and Eddie are going out of town." She mentioned her little bingo buddy. I knew my mother was dating and I tried to ignore it. From the outside looking in, you wouldn't have guessed she was dating.

Once a month was when she got dolled up and went out to dinner with her 'friend'.

She deserved happiness from the other sex, so I didn't get involved. My mother was grown and I was grown. Like she didn't pry too much into my business, I did the same and respected her space. When I suggested we all move into this house together, that was her fear. After promising I wouldn't get into her business, she agreed that we could move into this house together.

"I mean... I can watch them alone."

"You've raised one, so you know what you're doing." She pursed her lips.

"What's going on?" Happy came out of the room with her coffee mug. The girl went home and returned with a suitcase of things, including this coffee mug.

"Colt decided to watch his friend's eleven-year-old daughter and newborn son."

"Why would you volunteer for that?"

"They need to get away. I'm fine and can handle it."

"Well, I'll be here to help you," she assured me.

Kissing her on the cheek, I rubbed her shoulders. "Thank you, Hap."

My mother turned her back and went into the kitchen. "Bless their hearts, Lord," she tossed over her shoulders and went back to stirring the gumbo.

Happy and I went back into the room. "What are you doing for Christmas?" she randomly asked.

"Going to the mountains with the family."

"That sounds so fun."

"We've never been, so we figured it would be cool for the girls to experience."

"Am I invited?"

"Do you want to be invited?"

"Yes." She walked around the bed and pouted while tugging on my shirt. "You don't want to see what I could do in a cabin with whipped cream and a mistletoe?"

"Hmm, now I feel inclined to invite you just so I can find out."

"My family's Christmas party is coming up and I want to bring you."

"Happ—"

"I know what you're thinking. I've been avoiding having the conversation with Phil and it's been pretty easy because he hasn't reached out to me, besides sending me text messages that I ignored. I'm going to have the conversation with him, I just need more time." She cut me off before I could address what she had just explained.

"Look, I'm not gonna keep doing this for long. I get you and him were together for long and there's some things that you need to consider, but what about me? I feel like I have a voice in this, too."

"And you do, babe. I promise you do. Just give me some extra time to handle things. I think next week I'll go home and face everything I've been avoiding."

Kissing her on the lips, I nodded. "All right. For tonight, I want you next to me."

"Yes, sir." She giggled and gathered up her laptop and jumped on the bed. Falling on the bed, I rested my head on her thighs as she stroked my beard. It was my favorite thing that she did for me. The feeling of her small, smooth hands stroking my beard put me to sleep every time.

I jumped up out my sleep and looked at the clock on my night table. It was two in the morning. Happy was lying beside me, asleep. We had fallen asleep while she stroked my beard. Picking her up, I positioned her the correct way, then covered her up. Grabbing my phone, I went to the kitchen and guzzled a glass of water before disarming the alarm and going to sit on the back patio. Scrolling through my call log, I came across Azmina's number and sighed before pressing her name. The phone rang a few times before her groggy voice came across the line.

"Colt? Are you okay?" she questioned. "No, go back to bed," she whispered to someone in the background.

"Yea. I'm good. I just needed to talk to you real quick."

"I'm kinda on a date..." Her voice trailed off. I looked at my phone and shook my head. It was then that I realized Azmina played the innocent teacher role who wants to get married, have children and build a life. Truth be told, she wanted to fuck around with men until someone realized she possessed some good sex and wanted to lock that down.

"At two in the morning?"

"Listen, what did you call for?" Her tone changed. She went from being sleeping beauty to the damn wicked queen.

"You know what... nothing," I replied and ended the call. I didn't need to explain anything to her. I hit the block button on her name and went back inside. There was no need to have further conversation with her. If she continued to speak to my child about things other than school, she was going to find her way to the unemployment office. When I climbed back into bed, Happy snuggled closer to me and kissed me on the lips.

"Where did you go?"

"Get some water," I lied. "Go back to sleep."

"K. Love you."

"Love you too."

Chapter Fourteen

DEALING WITH THINGS HEAD ON

Happy

It was the second week of December and I was so into the holiday spirit. Both Colt and I decided it would be best for me to return home and deal with the things I had been avoiding. Except, I had been home one week and hadn't handled anything. Besides working, I came home and sat on the phone with Colt. If he was up in the air, then I would online shop or binge watch TV. Today, I was meeting my sister at her home to have lunch. I tried to get out of it and she forced me to swear that I would come. Kharisma had been busy with work and traveling from Savannah to Atlanta. We caught up with each other on the phone, but I felt like she was keeping something from me. Kharisma wasn't the type to sit and spill what was going on with her. She could be going through hell and would put a smile on her face every time you saw her. She was also the type of person you didn't push or pry into her business, although it was one of her favorite pastimes that she did to other people.

I pulled into her driveway and was about to turn my car off

when Phil's number came across my display screen in the car. Phil and I hadn't had one conversation. To me, the relationship was over. There was no need to try and fix things and make it right. After experiencing how a real man was supposed to love his family, I wanted no parts of the part-time love Phil had provided for the last four years. When he missed our anniversary, it was the last straw, or so I thought. The straw that broke the camel's back was how he didn't bother to continue calling me. This was the first time he had reached out since I had seen all his missed calls when I powered on my phone. Pressing the green icon button, I answered the call.

"Happy?"

"Yes."

"Babe, where have you been? I know you like your solitude, but don't go away on me like that. Your sister said you were in Dubai."

"I needed to get away."

"We need to talk about Thanksgiving. Why haven't you ever told me about what hap—"

"Let's not. It happened and I don't plan on revisiting it again."

"That's not fair."

"What's not fair? Did you get raped? Do you have to relive it every time you speak about it?"

The line grew quiet. I guess he was trying to gather his thoughts for his response. "Babe, I want to be here for you."

"And I appreciate that, I just don't want to talk about it."

"Well, I've missed you."

"Aw."

"Hap, why do you sound so dry?"

"Just tired. I've been working really hard."

"You gained more clients?"

"Yes. A lot of them saw my blog post when I was in Dubai, so they're booking me left and right."

"I wish we would have experienced that together. You went alone?"

"With a friend."

"A male?"

"Phil, what are you trying to ask me?"

"You've been distant and I want to make sure we're good." I didn't reply, so he continued talking. "I want you to have dinner with me next week at my parents' house. I also want you to coordinate our outfits for your parents' Christmas party."

"I'll see. I'm pretty swamped."

"Happy... it's just dinner. Please."

I felt like I kind of owed him that. "Fine."

"Okay, let me get back to work. I'll talk to you tonight, Sweetheart," he replied and quickly ended the call.

I killed my engine and got out the car. "No, you won't, I'll be on the phone with my baby," I replied and walked up the steps to Kharisma's house.

Since she knew I was on the way, she had the door already opened. She and Tommi lived in an exclusive gated community in Alpharetta. She could fall asleep with her door open and alarm disarmed and she would still be safe. When I was looking for a home, I had looked in her community. It was something for people about to settle down or with families. All the houses were too much for just me. Not to mention, Phil wasn't anywhere close to giving me a ring or a baby.

"Khar! I'm here," I called out and placed my Givenchy bowling bag on her oak foyer table. "You better have some good food, too!" I yelled out and went into the kitchen.

When I walked into the kitchen, Kharisma was sitting at the kitchen table with my mother. I rolled my eyes because I knew she would pull something like this. My mother's back was turned and Khar was the only one who saw my facial expression.

She forced me, she mouthed and I sighed.

"Hey, Happy!" Khar jumped up and kissed me. "Girl, you getting thicker... what you been eating?"

"Food. The food I thought you and me were only going to eat," I muttered.

"Stop. She wants to talk to you and forced me to invite you here," she whispered. "Let me go and check on the pool man... Last time, he put too much chlorine in the pool. Can y'all believe that?" She laughed her phony ass on out of the kitchen with the quickness.

My mother stood up and smiled. "My happiness..." She allowed her voice to trail off. "I've missed you. You had all of us worried."

"I needed time and I needed to get away."

"Understandable, but not even Phil was able to find you. Hap, we love you and just want to make sure you're safe."

"I'm here, mama. Not harmed and I'm safe."

She hugged me and pulled me back to kiss me on the forehead, then kissed me again. "I love you, Happy Joy."

"Love you too, mama."

My mother had told me to shut my mouth about the rape all these years. You would think that I would be angry, bitter and resentful against her. At one point, I was. When I couldn't focus because that was on my mind, or when she tried to get me fitted for Jade's wedding, I hated her. Over the years, I had to learn to forgive her. We had two definitions of protecting your family. She thought by sweeping things under the rug, it would make it go away, while I liked to deal with things head on to avoid hiding secrets. With therapy and time, I was able to forgive my mother. Did I forgive her for her? No, I did it because holding onto the hate I had for her was like drinking poison and expecting her to kneel over and die – it wasn't going to happen.

Kharisma peeked her head back in and felt it was safe to come in. I knew she was just doing what my mother had ordered her to. My mother had a way with words, and everyone usually fell head over heels for them and listened to her demands.

"Lunch is ready," she smiled.

"We're not eating in here?"

"No, I ordered food from our favorite restaurant, *Houston's*." She clapped her hands. "Come into the dining room."

My mother locked her hands in mine and we walked to the dining room. Kharisma had everything laid out with plates, silverware, the whole nine. We took our seats and said a quick prayer before digging into our food. I was surprised at how hungry I was. Being at Colt's, I had gotten used to Ms. Nia cooking and having a meal. If I didn't eat, she was the first to ask me if I had eaten anything. When I was home alone, I wasn't worried about eating and I didn't have anyone to remind me to feed my stomach. I cut into the salmon and took a bite. The juices fell into my mouth and I was so excited to get to the next piece.

"Who did you go the Dubai with?" my mother questioned me.

"My friend."

"Friend? Who?"

"His name is Colt Wright." Since I had planned to tell Phil after his dinner that we were over, I figured I'd better prepare my mother first. I was tired of hiding the love I had for Colt. She was going to meet him at the Christmas party anyway.

"A male?" She chewed with her hand over her mouth, like the proper southern belle. "You didn't tell me you had a gay friend."

"He's not gay."

"Straight? He knows you have a boyfriend," she countered.

"He does."

"Happy, why are you beating around the bush?"

"Mom, I've been having lots of sex with Colt Wright. We had so much sex in Dubai that the management knocked on the door for us to keep it down." Colt had a way with his tongue and he had me crying, screaming and shaking so loud that they had to warn us to keep it down.

The look on my mother's face should have been a funny Christmas card. I was almost tempted to snap a picture before she switched her expression. Kharisma snickered as she cut into her steak.

"Happy! You're in a relationship with Phil."

"Ma, am I? Phil is always so busy that we never spend time together. For years, I've been unhappy and didn't realize it. I was trying to do this for you. I wanted you to see that I was normal and could carry a real relationship after being raped."

"We'll not talk about that."

"Why, mama? I mean, it's just the three of us," Kharisma butted in. "I think a lot of stuff needs to be talked about."

She shook her head. "Oh, you think I have stuff that I don't want to talk about? Try *your* father." The way she said father didn't rub me the right way. For now, I ignored it.

"Happy was raped and you're acting like she scraped her knee or something. It should be talked about. She suffered for years doing what you asked her to do."

"Can you imagine if that got out?"

"Could you imagine being a mother and worrying about your daughter, not trying to hide secrets?"

"I've been more than a *mother.* A damn *mother* when I didn't want to be." She spoke with that tone again. I chalked it up to her being scared or even nervous to talk about the situation.

"Mama, I needed you and you basically told me to get over it. Did you ever stop to think about how I felt?"

"Girls... I was put in a bind, and as a mother and wife, I had to make the best choice for my family. Your father was rolling out his twenty-year campaign with Galleria stores, Jade and Tony were going to announce their engagement, and not to mention, the Blatimores had just donated to open the new store near the Perimeter Mall. Accusing Tony would have foiled all those plans."

"What about your daughter?" Kharisma yelled.

"I watched that tape and cried myself to sleep. Your father asked for months what was going on with me. I cried for you and watching how broken he made you, Happy, tore me up. I sat and saw how you struggled to go back to being normal. I prayed and prayed that my decision to keep quiet wasn't a bad one. Then, you met Phil. You were so happy with him and I watched how he was with you, so I figured a ring or baby would make you happier. So, I continued to put that in your ear as things you wanted."

"I want to be married and have children, just not with Phil. I realized that I don't want to marry a man like Phil. You want me to marry a man like Phil."

"I was born in Columbus, Georgia. We didn't have much and my mother always said that my looks would take me places. It took me right into the arms of your father, who promised me the world. Everything he had told me he would do, he has come through on. All he asked was for me to raise his babies, keep his house a home, and be his prayer warrior. I've done all those things and look how God has blessed our family. You girls have careers that girls would go in debt trying to achieve. Well, Kharisma does. However, you are well off. Look at this house, look at your townhome, and look at Jade's life. Often, we have to sacrifice things to get where we want to get in life."

"You really should have saved that pathetic story for yourself." Kharisma chewed on her steak and looked at our mother with disgust. "Fuck this life. My sister was raped, and if that meant we had to be middle class, lower class, and I had to take a loan out to go to medical school, then that's what we should have done. This woman." Her voice cracked. "Suffered rape and her abuser was flaunted around the damn family like a fucking show pony. And, here you sit with your diamonds, pearls and fur hung in my front closet, talking about sacrifices? You have never had to make a sacrifice, and even when God put one in your lap, you still picked your-damn-self!" Kharisma pushed her plate away and stormed out the room.

"That mouth of hers." My mother cut into her lamb, unbothered. "Happy, when I viewed that tape, I wasn't the same." She mentioned the tape again.

"Tape?"

"Yes, there are security tapes. With how much money your father's wine collection is, you didn't think he had security cameras?"

"Where are they?"

"Destroyed. I'm willing to go to therapy so we can work through this. I love you, baby girl. You're my baby girl."

I looked up at the ceiling to keep the tears from falling. She had proof that this monster raped me and had destroyed it. I thought I had forgiven her, but the hate seeped into my heart the way water seeped into a room during a flood.

"Do you hear me?"

I pushed my chair back and headed to find Kharisma. When I walked upstairs, I found her in the master bedroom. "I'm sorry, Happy. I tried, but I lost it."

Pulling her into my arms, we hugged tightly. "Thank you."

"I love you, Happy. If Colt makes you happy, then you should be with him. The smile that crossed your face when you mentioned his name let me know you're happy."

"He makes me so happy."

"Then he's who you should be with. Don't listen to Mom, and don't be like me and Jade. Be with someone who *makes your heart run wild.*"

I hugged her once more and headed downstairs. My mother was sitting at the dining room table, finishing her meal. "You girls really need to come finish this food."

"Bye, mom. I'll see you at the Christmas party," I replied, heading to the front to grab my purse and leave.

Who knew if my mother and I would ever come back from this. Right now, she wasn't my focus. Karma was one woman you didn't piss off with consequences.

I didn't want to be here at all, sitting in the front seat of Phil's car, on our way to this dinner. I didn't want to be here nor there. While I was counting down the time until he dropped me back home, he was happy, singing and holding my hand. To Phil, everything was right in his world. It was one of the reasons I realized both he and I could never be. My feelings were nonexistent to him. The only reason he felt like we should talk about me being rape was because it was brought up. If he didn't bring it up, he would look like a douche bag who didn't care.

"It feels good being together again. It's been a while since we've done anything together. That's about to change, too."

"Really?"

"Yes. I realized that I need to be there for you more. You need me and I've been choosing my work over you." It sounded like he had a long and detailed talk with my mother. I wouldn't put it past my mother to get on her phone and tell Phil that he needed to step his game up with me. Little did she know, I was done and over the whole relationship.

"Sounds nice," I replied as we pulled into his parents' driveway. He killed the engine and turned his attention to me.

"Tonight is about us. I want to make you so happy, babe. I really do."

Giving him a smile, he got out and opened the door for me. I was wearing a Cashmere beige sweater dress with a pair of thigh-high Gucci monogram canvas heels.

We walked into his parents' house and everyone was there. His older brother with his wife and their two teenage daughters were there, along with his aunt and her new husband. Kenya came out of the kitchen and hugged me tightly.

"I haven't seen you since your birthday. How are you, love?"

"I'm great. It smells delicious. Phil didn't tell me you would be cooking, I would have come earlier."

"I've hired the best caterer in Atlanta to cook for us tonight. She has some amazing food brewing in there. Come, let me get you a drink."

"I'll take some water."

"No champagne?"

"No, I'm fine... just some water." Just the mention of champagne sent chills down my throat. I had never drunk champagne since that night. If it was a celebration, I always opted for wine or something stronger. Long as I didn't have to hold a champagne flute, I was fine.

Cabin trip canceled. They overbooked us.

I saw the message from Colt. The cabin trip was something I was actually looking forward to.

"Here you go, baby. So, how's everything with Happy G?"

"Great. I'm just working and continuing to work."

"Hmm, I see you're working my son, too," she laughed. "I see that passion mark you're trying to hide. I just love you two together."

My face turned red because I hadn't realized I had a hickie. Colt must have put that on my neck during our lovemaking. If Kenya knew, she would have known that her son hadn't touched me in months.

Offering a weak smile, I switched subjects. "What's the celebration?"

"Well, Phil was waiting to tell you, but I guess I should let the cat out the bag. "Phil made partner!" she announced.

"Really?" I was legit happy for him. Even though he was shit as a lover and boyfriend, there was no denying how hard he had worked to make partner. "I'm so happy for him."

"Yes, girl. It may not be with the family's firm, but he's making strides in his field and I'm happy for him."

"Me too. Let me go find him." I quickly excused myself and went to look for Phil. I couldn't find him but had got caught up in a conversation with his sister-in-law. She loved fashion, too, and had great conversation. I didn't remember what she said she did because that was how uninterested I was with his family. We exchanged cards as we got further caught into our conversation over this season's Balenciaga.

It was an hour into the party and Kenya was calling everyone to the dining room. I took this as my moment to look for Phil. I searched downstairs until I eventually headed upstairs and looked through the rooms.

"Hmm, shit, right in the back of your throat," I heard. I followed Phil's voice and found him getting a blow job from his assistant. Quietly stepping back, I went downstairs and sat down and waited for him to come down.

Everyone was seated and being served when Phil finally must have busted his nut and came downstairs. He sat next to me and smiled before kissing me on the cheek. I wanted to slap his lips off of his face. How could I really be mad? I was cheating on him, too, but I felt mine was justified. Phil ignored me, we didn't have sex or even date, and all of that wasn't because of me. So, while I was struggling with trying to make us work, he was busy having sex with his assistant.

"I want to thank everyone for coming to celebrate this with us. Philly, I'm so happy for you." Kenya stood up and looked at her son.

"Thanks, mama. I appreciate you all for coming out. This has been a long time in the making and I'm happy it's finally here."

"We all are. Congratulations, Phil," I smiled.

"Thanks, love. You deserve the world because you've been on this journey more than anyone else."

"Well, I can't disagree with that. I've spent many nights alone," I chuckled. It was so hard trying to play phony in front of everyone. Even with what I had seen him doing, I couldn't sit here and act a fool. My family's name depended on my actions and I didn't want to give them the wrong impression on what kind of woman I was.

"That's all about to stop, honey. I want us to find a home together and I want you to be my wife." He stood up and pulled a velvet purple box from his slacks.

Phil got on one knee and pulled the ring out. "Will you give me the honor of becoming my wife, Happy Galleria?" The whole table gasped, clapped, and spoke amongst themselves.

For years, I had pictured this moment in my sleep, shower, and even at work. I just knew this would be special. I would cry and mess up my makeup while accepting the ring, then I would bend down and kiss him on the lips and we would both taste the salt from my tears. After, we would go home and make passionate love to each other while I stared at my beautiful ring. This wasn't that moment and I was actually sick to my stomach watching him on the floor with this ring.

"Happy, you better tell that man," Kendra squealed.

My mind told me to take the ring, smile and continue with dinner, then tell him later. My heart told me something different. This man proposed to me because he finally made partner. He made me wait and waste some of my good years for his own selfish gain. It wasn't until he got what he wanted that he was ready to finally give me what I wanted.

"I can't." I stood up and walked out of the dining room, then the house. I heard everyone whisper what and why I was leaving. My spirit would not allow me to accept this ring. Even under false pretenses. My ring finger deserved to have a ring on it from someone who loved, cared and wanted to marry me. How could he want to marry me when he was just getting a blow job from another woman a couple minutes ago? Accepting his ring and marrying him would just set me up for a sad, lonely and miserable marriage.

Phil came flying out the house right behind me. "What the hell was that about, Happy?"

"I can't go through with marrying you."

"For years, you've spoken about marriage, we've got into arguments about it, and the moment I finally do it, you're talking about you *can't.*"

"I know about you and your assistant."

You would think the asshole's face would show some regret. "So? It's nothing between us. She sucks me off when I'm stressed."

"Do you hear yourself?"

"Do you hear yourself?" he repeated. "Happy, I'm finally ready to settle down and give you what you want."

"See, there's two things with what you said."

"What?" He was honestly confused on what he said, which was sad.

"You're finally ready after you've done what you wanted. And give me what I *want?* Are you kidding me?"

"Is this about the guy you slept with? Because you're pointing the blame and you've been being a little slut on the low, too. Your mother called and told me."

"So is this why you decided to give me that ugly-ass ring?"

"It's my great grandmother's ring."

"And it's ugly."

"Whatever. And no, I had my mother pull it from the safety deposit box months ago. I knew I was going to make partner and wanted to propose the same night I found out. I've always known I wanted to marry you, I just wanted to prove to my father that I could have it all without him." His face softened.

"Phil, you showed your father that you can't have it all. Your parents are still together and your father has built the most known law firm in Georgia. You see the way he looks at your mother? He loves her and I bet he didn't make her wait like a child for a ring."

He shoved his hands inside of his pocket. "You're right. I shouldn't have done that to you. I also knew doing that would distract me from my goal."

"Well, you accomplished one goal and lost another one. We both know that this isn't going to work. I'm not happy and you're not either. Look at us, we don't even know each other. Four years and a whole lot of work and we could barely come up with a conversation on the ride over here."

He laughed slightly. "You're right."

"Oh, I know."

"Hap, you're an amazing woman. Any man, even the man you cheated on me with, is lucky to have you. I just wish I would have realized that before I pushed you away. Getting down on my knee at your birthday dinner months ago was what I should have done. Instead, I was selfish and worried about my career and thinking a fiancée would deter me from my ultimate goal."

I walked over and touched his face. "You've accomplished it. Now, accomplish love and experience what it's like to be so in love that you feel your head is going to spin." On my way out, I had quickly logged into my Uber app and ordered an Uber. A black Tahoe with tinted windows pulled to the curb. "This is me."

"Take care of yourself, Hap."

I smiled and dug into my purse. Taking his key out the fancy box he had given it to me in for my birthday, I handed it to him. "I believe this belongs to you."

"Thank you." We hugged and I got into my Uber and headed right to be in Colt's arms.

Chapter Fifteen

ARE WE READY FOR THIS?

Colt

When I offered to watch Darrius' and Kelli's kids, I didn't know how hard it would be. Mama was gone, so it was only Happy and I holding down the fort. I should say, Darrius' and Kelli's son. Milani was an angel like she usually was and helped out as much as Happy and I allowed her to. The girls were obsessed with trying to take care of Miles. It had been a while since I had to deal with a newborn, and Miles had me second guessing if I wanted any more children. It was Happy who surprised me. She coddled him, sang to him and did his night feedings while I laid on the floor, trying to find my sanity. One day, she was going to make an amazing mother. I loved how she loved on Miles, Milani, and River. She took control of the kitchen while Mama was gone and we hadn't missed one meal. The house was cleaned, and when I had to fly to New York and back for work, she held down the fort without me.

I remember her mentioning she wanted to be a wife, a mother and have a family, and I could see why. She did everything so effortlessly and made it seem so easy. Even with her working, she would bring Miles with her to meetings. When Darrius and Kelli came back, you could see the glow on their faces. That was what made it all worth the late nights and early mornings with Miles. Both of them needed this time away to reconnect with each other and remember why they had fallen in love in the first place. Children were blessings, but they also had the ability to break us apart. Parents had to remember that kids grew up and eventually moved away and started their own families. One day, Miles and Milani would move out and live their own lives. Happy didn't want to give Miles back and was a little depressed after he left.

She told me that she had ended things with Phil, and they ended on good terms. I was glad that I could finally call her mine. It was so crazy that I wasn't looking for anyone and then Happy Galleria bumped into my life – literally. This woman made me so happy, I felt like my soul was on fire. Every morning when I woke up next to her, I knew it was going to be a good day. The way she not only cared for me but for my family, too, was another thing. She and my mother would sit in the kitchen for hours, talking about nothing in particular. River loved everything about Happy and loved that she now styled her for school. According to her, she was the most stylish girl in her elementary school. It was crazy, but I liked to think that Tamia had sent her to me. She knew I was silently drowning and she sent a life vest by the name of Happy to bring me to surface.

"Babe, I'm sorry that call ran too long," Happy apologized as I drove.

"You're good... everything good?"

"More than good. Remember Phil's sister-in-law?"

"You mentioned her."

"At his parents' house a few weeks ago?"

"Yeah, I remember, what happened with her?"

"Maybe you should pull over to the side of the road for this one."

I looked at her like she was crazy. "Happy, tell me the damn news."

"Sheesh... I'll just tell you."

"Happy, tell me."

"Okay, she's the creative director for Vogue!" She screamed so loud. I should have pulled over because she scared me when she yelled.

"That's great... What does that mean?"

"Well, she told me that she has been following my blog for a while now, and she always tried to bring it up whenever we were over Phil's parents' home, but the last few times I wasn't there. She asked me to come along and help her style some models for this exclusive fashion week just for the shareholders for the company."

"Baby, that's amazing! I'm so proud of you!" I raised my voice now. This was all she had been talking about since we'd met. Hearing news like this made me feel much better about going to this Christmas party we were on our way to.

"Thank you. She's sending me over the vision and she wants me to send her a PowerPoint presentation on what I would do differently."

"We should just skip the pa—"

"Nope! I want you to meet my sister."

"Not sisters?"

"No. I haven't spoken to Jade since Thanksgiving and I don't expect to either. Jade runs from conflict, so I wouldn't expect anything else."

"Wow, I hate that for you."

"Me too, but if she wants to still remain married to her rapist of a husband, she can leave me alone."

"I feel you."

"Anyway, this is good news. I feel like so much good news is coming into my life since I opened up my heart."

"What other good news you got?"

"Everything, babe." She smiled at me. The theme for the party was ugly Christmas sweater. I didn't know how she could make an ugly Christmas sweater look good, but she did. We wore matching sweaters.

We arrived at her family's home and the doors were opened for us. They had valet take my car while Happy and I made our way inside. The decorations were like something out of the white house. You could tell someone had taken time and precision to put these up.

"You grew up here?"

"Yep." She smiled as we walked inside, holding hands.

"I grew up in a two-bedroom apartment with a roach name Ed."

"Babe, stop." She laughed loudly. "Khar should be somewhere." We walked further into the house.

They gave us red martinis when we made it into the sitting room. Happy spotted her sister, talking to her husband. She pulled us over to them and hugged her sister.

"Hap, if I would have known you was going to kill this outfit, I wouldn't have come." Her sister laughed. "How do you make a sweater as ugly as that look so good?"

"That's the same thing Colt told me. Tommi, this is my boyfriend, Colt," she introduced us. Dude flicked his wrist, then shook my hand.

"Hey, Colt... I'm glad Happy found someone who makes her happy... no pun intended." He started laughing.

"Colt, this is my sister, Kharisma Galleria," she introduced us.

"I feel like I know you." She hugged me. "Thank you for loving my sister the way you do. She tells me everything and I appreciate you caring for her the way you do."

"I love your sister. She's my world, and I would have never pushed my way into her life if I had no plans of doing right by her."

"Thank you." She gently patted my shoulder. I watched as she turned her attention to her sister. "You saw Mama yet?"

Happy nodded her head no. "Honestly, if I went this entire party and didn't see her, I would be satisfied. I do want to see Daddy, you know where he is?"

"He should be somewhere around here. Last I saw him, he was

trying to stay away while talking to one of Mama's friends. You know he can't stand none of her friends."

"He does better than me with pretending to pay attention."

"Oh! Before you get lost in the party, me and Tommi want to invite both of you to our home for a small get-together."

"Sure, you know I love coming to your house, especially when you're not ambushing me."

"Mama forced me," Kharisma laughed. "Anyway, it's on Christmas Eve. I know you mentioned you have a daughter and mom, so please bring them. Dress fancy, too." She turned her attention to me, then back to Happy.

"Thank you for inviting me and my family."

"You're family now. Anybody who makes my little sister as happy as you have been is family to me. I can't promise my mother will be accepting."

"I'm well prepared."

"And my dad, he's cool, so I'm sure he'll be down."

"Thanks for the tips."

Happy grabbed my hand and we walked around the party. A few people stopped her and she introduced me to them as her boyfriend. While we were talking to one of her aunts, she spotted her father grabbing some wine from the server and rushed over to him.

"Daddy!" she squealed.

You could tell the love this man had for his daughter. He wore a somber look before she called his name, but once he laid eyes on her, his face lit up and he smiled so brightly. Happy let go of my hand and ran into her father's arms. She had mentioned how she hadn't spoken to or seen her father since Thanksgiving, and she hated herself for it.

"Hap, I didn't think you were coming." He hugged her tightly, then looked up at me. "What do we have here?"

I extended my hand out and replied, "How are you doing, Mr. Galleria? My name is Colt Wright and I'm Happy's boyfriend." We shook hands and he looked down at Happy.

"Firm handshake," he commented on my handshake. "What do you do, son?"

"I'm a pilot for Delta airlines, Sir."

"Babe, don't be too humble. He's a captain, daddy," Happy mentioned.

His father raised his eyebrow. "A black pilot, I like it. Boyfriend? What happened to Phil?" Happy looked down and her father lifted her face. "I know Phil didn't make you happy. I also know that you tried as long as you did for your mother. Me and your mother are going through some issues and counseling because of what she hid from me. As far as Tony, I'm working on tr—"

"Daddy, don't get involved. Tony will have to pay for what he has done. I don't want to relive any of it anymore. I'm happy and I just want to move forward with my life. I even forgive Jade for still being married to him. I just want to move forward with love and light."

He kissed her on the forehead. "With love and light, baby. Love and light," he repeated. "If you make my baby girl as happy as she says you do, then you're good in my bo—"

"Happy, I didn't know you were coming." Who I assumed was her mother came over and forced Happy into a hug.

"Hi, mama." Happy greeted her mother.

"And who is th—"

"My boyfriend," Happy cut her off.

"How are you, Mrs. Galleria? My name is Colt Wright."

"Oh, I know who you are. The man who allowed my daugh—"

"Diana, this is not the time nor the place for this. This is who Happy wants to be with and I'm fine with it. We need to respect her choices, and if this is what she wants, I'm supporting her full force."

"Thank you, Daddy." Happy kissed her father on the cheek.

"Mama, I'm just gonna make it clear that I'm happy, in love, and me and Colt are together. Get used to seeing him and his family wherever I am. If you'll excuse me, I'm going to grab something to eat because I'm starving."

"I told you about not eating during the day, babe," I reminded her. She got so busy that she often forgot to feed herself, then suffered hunger headaches because of it.

"See, I like this man already. Welcome to the family, Colt. Call me if you need anything." Her father shook my hand again.

Happy and I found some food and a small cocktail table to stand and eat at. "That went well."

"My mother had no choice. I knew my father would be happy because he doesn't care about how much a man makes or anything like that. He's more concerned about a man having a job. My mother is the one who cares about a man's status."

"Speaking about status... what's up with your sister's husband?"

"Ehh, he's flamboyant... I guess," she replied.

"Okay."

"Babe, stop being shady."

"Man, all I'm doing is trying to find out some things." I stuffed a crab puff into my mouth. "You having a good time?"

"Actually... I am. I'm glad you decided to come."

"Decided?"

"Okay, okay, I kinda forced you."

"I'm glad you know," I replied and reached across the table and kissed her on the lips. "You make my world spin, Happy G."

"You're my world, Colt Wright."

Christmas Eve

Since I was at my max hours for the year, I wasn't working. To keep my flying sharp, I went to the Gwinnett County Airport and flew a few times a week. Having more time to spend at home felt nice, especially with the long list of gifts River had requested. I spent most of the month buying gifts, spending time with Mama, and getting whatever time I could get with Happy. She was busy doing her presentation for the creative director and styling the clients she did have. We decided that we would stay at each other's places a few nights a week. This week was my week to stay at her townhouse. Her house was nice and you could tell she spent money to decorate it the way she wanted. I also understood why she hated being home alone. It was a lot of house for just one person. Since Kharisma's Christmas Eve get-together was today, Happy had invited us all to stay at her townhouse.

"Happy, what kind of coffee maker is this? I want some coffee before we head out."

"Ms. Nia, that's a cappuccino machine," Happy giggled. "We can stop at Starbucks before we get to Khar's house," she told her.

"Okay."

"I love our outfits, Happy." River spun around with her navy blue dress that had a satin bow towards the back. Mama wore a halter top dress that was the same color and stopped at her knees. Happy paired the outfit with a pair of heels that matched the dress.

"Me too... I feel so sexy." Mama spun around with River. "Thank you, Happy."

"You both look stunning," Happy complimented as she put her earrings in her ear. Happy wore a navy blue silk wrap dress that dropped to the floor. The neckline fell to the middle of her breasts. She looked fine and I wanted to rip the dress right off her body as soon as we stepped into the house later on.

"All my ladies look beautiful. I'm lucky."

"Thanks, babe." Happy kissed me. "You look handsome." I wore a pair of Khaki slacks, Versace loafers, and a navy blue silk dress shirt.

We all piled into the car and I drove over to Kharisma's house. My mother told us to forget about her coffee because she was ready for something a little stronger. It didn't take long to get to Khar's house, and when we had to be buzzed into the gate by security, I wished I could have said I was surprised. When we drove through the neighborhood, you could tell they spent money on their landscape and HOA fees. Hell, I paid five hundred dollars a year, so I knew theirs had to be at least tripled.

"This one right here," Happy pointed out.

I pulled into the driveway and hopped out to open their doors. Happy held my hand and we walked inside the house. The house was decorated in white. Everything was white and gray. The servers were dressed in all white and there were only a few people there. Thankfully, it wasn't like the Christmas party, and I didn't have to meet a bunch of people. Happy's parents greeted us as soon as we walked in. I shook their hands and introduced them to my mother and River.

"Do you know what she's doing?" Happy's mother asked. It seemed like she was dying to know what her older daughter had planned.

"Nope, but where is she?"

"Upstairs. I tried to go in and she told me she was waiting for you to come."

Happy excused herself and went upstairs. Mama, River, and I went and sat down in the large sitting room. My mom was snapping pictures of her and River, then forced me to take a selfie with them. "Happy has me feeling myself," she laughed.

My mother did look amazing, and it was nice to see her dressed up and enjoying herself for once. Even River was excited about her dress and the fact that she got to wear makeup today. There was a wooden chair next to the white couch. Diana, Happy's mother, came and sat down next to me.

"I just wanted to come and talk to you. We didn't get a chance to talk at the Christmas party."

"Yeah, it was pretty busy and not the place."

"Exactly. Where do you see you and my daughter going? You know she's gonna be thirty next year and the things she wants, right?"

"I'm aware."

"Where's your cell phone?" I pulled out my cell phone and held it up. She took my phone and programmed her number into my phone. "I called myself so I have your number. Despite what you have heard about me, I love my daughters. Some of my decisions haven't been the best, but I truly want the best for each of them."

"As a mother should. Proposing and getting married is something I'm gonna do on my terms. Happy is gonna be thirty, and I'm already in my thirties. Age has nothing to do with our future, it's more so our feelings for each other. Happy knows that I'm not the type who is going to ask her to marry her because she wants it. We got this."

"Her last boyfriend let me be involved in everything that had to do with their future."

"Maybe that's why her last relationship didn't last. No disrespect, Ms. Diana, but I'm a grown man. I'm not playing a high school kid's game. I know what I want and I know what I'm going to do. As far as a ring, yeah, I'll allow you to *help* me, but anything else, it's up to me." I could tell she didn't like what I had said.

"Colt, you're gonna have to learn that I get my way." She winked and patted me on the shoulder before she got up and walked out of the room.

"That woman is something else," my mother whispered. "Why is she so concerned about what you and Happy are doing?"

"Ma, she seems like she in all her daughters' business."

"I can see. The dad is over there sucking down his sixth drink. The man can barely stand." My mother was the type who observed everything. She watched her surroundings, then came to her decision about the person.

Happy came down and stood at the bottom of the circular staircase. She had a smile on her face as she clasped her hands together. "Thank you, everyone, for coming out tonight. There is only a small amount of you because both Tommi and Khar felt like you were all important to their relationship and have always shown support. A lot of you are probably asking why you're here and what's going on. Well, I'm here to tell you that you're here to attend the wedding of Tommi Blatimore and Kharisma Galleria," she announced and clapped her hands.

Everyone clapped while others gasped. Diana's face looked less than pleased while Paul, Happy's father, was clapping. "A wedding?

This is where the wedding is going to be?" Diana stood up and asked.

"Mama, this isn't about you." Happy laughed while looking around the room. "Sit down because the couple is coming down."

We all stood as the couple walked down, hand in hand. Kharisma had a white, sleek satin dress and Tommi had on a white suit. His shoes were blinged out with studs. Kharisma smiled as she came down the stairs. I wondered who Tommi's parents were, or if they were even here. The officiant turned out to be Kharisma's college best friend. Happy sat in the chair beside the couch I was seated on and we watched them get married. Happy wiped tears from her eyes as she watched her big sister get married. Even Mama got choked up and had to borrow some tissue from Happy to dab her eyes. The ceremony was beautiful and you could tell that these two loved each other. I loved that they decided to get married on their terms, not their parents'. The fact that it was a surprise and her mother couldn't stop her or add her two cents made it that more special.

In the backyard, there was a heated tent with tables, a dance floor, and food. Kharisma finally made it over to our table and she hugged each of us with the biggest smile on her face. "Thank you for coming. And nice meeting you, Ms. Nia. My sister has told me so much about you."

"Aw, nice to meet you, too, baby. And congratulations, you look beautiful."

"Like a princess," River added.

"Thank you, pretty girl."

We ate, danced and partied into the night with Tommi and Kharisma. Eventually, her parents left, but the party continued. Everyone had a good time and I was appreciative that Khar had invited both my mother and River along, too. At the end of the night, Happy and I got on the dance floor and danced to Major's "Why I Love You". When we got to the point of talking about marriage, I wanted to dance to this at our wedding. I stared into her eyes as she stared up at me. There was no one else on the dance floor with us. Everyone was sitting at their table, watching us dance. Kharisma was sitting on Tommi's lap, crying as she watched us. I saw her mouth that she loved Happy. If I could freeze this moment, I would.

"This is why I love you, because you looveeee me," Happy sang as she stared into my eyes. I bent down and kissed her on the lips and continued to dance the night away.

Christmas Morning

We ended up leaving the wedding around three in the morning. I was still laying in Happy's bed when she came into the room with a small box wrapped for me. I leaned up and accepted the box as she climbed into the bed beside me.

"Baby, I wanted to give you this gift this morning." She smiled and sat there and waited for me to open the box.

As I opened the box, I stared at her. "Anybody else up?"

"I tried to wake them up and your mama told me she was gonna get evil if I didn't leave her alone."

"Well, she shouldn't have been breaking down the floor with your father before they left," I chuckled. The DJ played some seventies music and both Paul and my mother got on the dance floor and danced for six songs straight. Diana sat at the table with a pout on her face because obviously, she wasn't getting her way and felt a way.

"I told her that and she tossed a pillow at me," she giggled. "And River said she doesn't need to wake up because her gifts are at her home, not here."

"She's right. We can get ready to head there because I know she'll be asking about going home soon."

"Can you open one of your gifts now?"

"All right, all right." I continued to pull at the wrapping paper. I could tell it was a chain of some sort based off the box. I opened the top of the box and looked at Happy. "Are you serious?"

"I found out a few weeks ago... and wanted to wait to tell you, you know."

"You're fucking pregnant." I tossed the box and grabbed her up. "You're pregnant!" I hollered loud as hell. I knew her neighbors heard.

She smiled and nodded. "I'm having your baby." She smiled wide.

It didn't take long for my mother and River to come busting into the room. "What did I just hear?"

"Happy is pregnant with my baby. My baby is having my baby!" I continued to laugh.

My mother clapped her hands together and put them to her mouth with tears in her eyes. "God, You are answering my prayers. God bless you both, this baby and our family."

"Our family is growing... I want a little brother!" River climbed up on the bed and hugged Happy around the neck. "I'm so happy my mommy sent you to my daddy," she whispered in her ear and Happy broke down crying. "I didn't want you to cry." River thought she said something wrong.

"No, these are tears of joy. I just love you all and feel so blessed that you guys have welcomed me into your family."

We all got on the bed and hugged each other tightly. I was blessed beyond measure. God had blessed me more than he could have ever. I wasn't worried about how long we'd known each other, if we would last, or any of those things. I knew that Happy was sent to me and that we would weather any storm that came our way. My family was growing and I felt like I had won the lottery. When I would pray to just be happy, I never imagined that God would actually send me a woman named Happy. God had a sense of humor and I was laughing and being grateful for all the blessings He was giving me. I wasn't worthy, but He deemed me worthy. And for that, I was going to always take care of my family.

EPILOGUE

A New Year, New Blessings

Happy

The last place I thought I would ever be was sitting front row at a Vogue private fashion week show. I wore a thick pair of Celine shades, Dior beige trench coat dress, thigh-high Alia boots, and a matching purse. I sat there with my legs crossed, watching all the models walk the runway. I remember when I used to sit and daydream about the day it would be my turn to style fashion shows and take control of things. As I sat down and swung my leg, I kept a poker face as I knew paparazzi were all over and if I had a mean mug, my mother wouldn't be pleased. I continued to watch the show and made note of things that I might want to add to my own personal collection. Models walked down the runway for the last time and bowed gracefully. Under my trench coat was my small baby bump. It poked out more these days. I was almost going to be four months soon. As soon as the models turned to walk to the back, I rose and sauntered toward the exit. I had flown to New York along with Mama Nia and River. They were visiting family while I came to sit at this fashion show. Colt was back to work and

I missed the hell out of him. We were in the process of figuring out the living situation. I was going to put my townhome up for rent and move in with Colt, but he was thinking of moving into something bigger. As long as I was next to him, I didn't care if we lived in a box.

"Happy G?" I heard my name being called and slowly turned around. I was faced with a short girl with flawless brown skin. Her natural hair was thick and curly and pushed back into a neat ponytail. She wore the latest Alexander McQueen boots and held a crocodile Birkin on her right arm.

"Yes?" It was so crazy how people called me Happy G in the streets now. While getting coffee, I would get stopped and asked what shoe they should wear on a date, or if their outfit was fine for the day. I was somebody on social media now. I guess I'd always been, but the outpouring had been more since I was with the editor in chief for Vogue on her Instagram.

"My name is Geisha. I love your blog. I constantly stalk your blog and Instagram for your outfit of the day." She gushed over my social media presence.

"Aw. Thank you. I appreciate the support." I turned quickly and tried to continue out of the venue, but I felt her hand on my trench.

"I wanted to talk to you about something, if you don't mind."

Turning back around, I smiled. "Sure, what's up?"

"Sorry. I could see you're on your way out, but I just felt this was my only chance. My uncle is West Platinum. He's been looking for a stylist and I think you're perfect for him."

West Platinum. As soon as his name came out of her mouth, I was sold on whatever she wanted to sell me. I wanted, no, I *needed* to know more about what she needed or wanted from me.

"West Platinum? You work for him?"

"Yes, it was either business school or working with my uncle. I chose my uncle because I could learn way more from him than from sitting in class with a man who has never touched a million dollars."

She had a point. West Platinum was a mogul. His name was on everything and everything he or his family touched turned to Platinum. Luckily for me, I followed his career. He started out as a rapper, took a step back from that and decided to launch his own music streaming app, which was worth millions, and now he was stepping back from rapping to run his family's record label, Platinum records. That man was on three Forbes covers and every magazine in-between.

"You have a point."

"Thanks. Well, my uncle's last stylist took a job overseas and he's in need of a new one. Not that he can't dress, but he's invited to all these red carpet events and I'm tired of him showing up looking like the fourth member of the Migos," she laughed. She was funny. Very funny.

"Who is he working with now?"

"I dislike the new stylist so bad that I never learned his name. He doesn't understand that my uncle is... well... old." She spat out the three letter word that the entire world dreaded hearing.

"Your uncle is in his thirties, that's not old."

"Thirty-four is old," she assured me.

"Does he know you're scouting for a new stylist?"

She switched her purse to her other hand and smirked. "Not exactly. When I saw you walk in, I knew I had to stop and talk to you."

"Your uncle may not want a new stylist."

"Oh, he does. He questions his outfit choices all the time. He's busy, so he really doesn't have the time to sit and pick out his own clothes."

"I have no problem meeting with your uncle." She grew excited and I held my hand up. "Under one condition: you let him know beforehand. I don't want to be a part of an ambush."

"I will." She pulled her iPhone out. "He just moved to Atlanta, and I know you live in Atlanta, so I can set something up for when you get back."

"Yes, just shoot me an email and we can get this going." A

client like West Platinum would mean more exposure than ever. Everyone knew West and loved him. If I styled him, that would be the ultimate client. I got excited thinking of all the clothes I could pull for him. "Thanks for thinking of me."

"No, thank you. I'm standing in front of Happy G. I'm excited you even took the chance to talk to me this long." She handed me her phone.

While I put the address to the hotel into the Uber app, I spoke. "Your uncle is West Platinum and you're being a fan over me?"

"It's different. Uncle Wes has been my uncle my entire life. So, he's always been Uncle Wes. I know who he is and what he does, but that doesn't change the fact that he's the man who practically raised me when my father died," she smiled. He has a heart. I could tell she was young, so I assumed she had to be nineteen or twenty at the oldest. I was intrigued. Styling West Platinum would be like a dream come true

We exchanged contact information and went our own way. I was so happy to get back to my hotel. Running a bath, I soaked in the tub, then called Colt, praying I caught him in time before he took off. "Hey, baby. I was just about to power my phone off."

"And you weren't going to call me?"

"I called Mama and told her the message I wanted her to give you."

"Aw."

"How did the show go?"

"It was great. You'll never guess whose niece I ran into."

"Who?"

"West Platinum."

"For real? I heard he just moved to Atlanta, too. Landing him as a client would be a big one."

"Right? I'm supposed to meet with him when I get back home."

"I'm proud of you, baby."

"Thank you."

"I'll see you when you guys get back. Love you, Happy G."

"I love you, too, Colt. Well, we love you, Colt Wright."

"I love you too. Can't wait to rub that belly when I touch down."

"We can't wait for you to rub it, too. Safe flight, baby."

"Thank you," he replied and we ended the call.

I sat in a tub at the Roosevelt hotel, feeling so special, blessed and everything else. God saw me fit to carry life into this world. My plan when I was younger was to be married, have a career and then have my children. Even up until a few months ago that was still my plan. It took Colt Wright to stumble into my life to show me that we couldn't plan our futures. I had a whole plan for everything and look at me now. Phil and I weren't together and I was now pregnant with Colt's baby, planning a future with him. Instead of getting the things I asked for, God gave me what He felt I needed the most. I needed a man... a real man like Colt, and he came with his own set of baggage, but I did, too. We both knew how to deal with each other and that was why I loved him. Love like this didn't come around too often, and when it did, you needed to grab it, hold tight, and never let it go. For years, I remained emotionless. For the first time in life, I was feeling and showing emotions and it felt *Wright.*

THE END

Book 2, Is There More? will be available soon.

(Kharisma's story)